A Room Full Of Keys

Richard A. Powell II

DEDICATION

If you are reading this book then it's dedicated to you. Thank you for taking a chance. Every writer needs readers, otherwise, we'd just be talking to ourselves, and I think we can all agree, that would be a little weird.

www.richardapowellii.com

Other works by Richard A. Powell II:

Kill Academy: Kill Series – Book One (2017)
RejectGuy99 (2015)
A Room Full of Keys (2013)
Neither Snow, Nor Rain, Nor Zombie Infection & Other Strange Tales (2012)

Available by order at bookstores and online worldwide

Regret for the things we did can be tempered by time;
it is regret for the things we did not do that is inconsolable.

- Sydney J. Harris

1

Saturday, November 7th, 1992 – 3:38 p.m.
Rural Ingham County, Michigan

The dank air smelled of rust and sweat and wood. The only light crept through the left edge of a single window above a decrepit farm sink, once pearly and glimmering but now charcoaled and covered in mildew. The cabin floor, made of three-inch wide oak planks, buckled in many places from the years of moist conditions and no repair. Many of the floor boards were also cracked and splintered, bare feet ill-advised.

Each of the four walls measured twenty-five feet wide and eight feet tall, with a lone door in the middle of the south wall. The core of the door was entirely oak but the outer layer was sheeted in steel with giant rivets along the middle and the edges. The steel had become heavily dimpled over time and streaks of watery rust overspread nearly seventy-five percent of the surface. The doorknob, a rich, emerald glass antique stolen from a furniture warehouse, emerged from the darkness like a beacon calling the ships to shore. It shadowed a large keyhole fit only for a well-patinaed skeleton key.

A plastic, battery-operated ivory kitchen clock hung above the door, the clear cover frosted over with condensation but always ticking away with a loud, deep, rhythmic cluck. Regardless of the timepiece and its noise, in that cabin, the universe stood still, even when the lock clicked and the knob turned, even when the devil stepped in to enact his version of hell on Earth.

The room was split into two irregular sides by a ragged bamboo room divider. The west side, farthest from the sink and equaling about one-third of the space, contained three stained and tattered twin-size mattresses, all resting side by side and touching. In the middle of the larger space, about five feet from the farm sink, was a forty-eight-inch-wide, round dining room table with only two chairs, oak in material, chipped and scratched with a faded dark brown finish.

The cabin lacked a bathroom, a white bucket near the corner of the room divider served that purpose. Filthy well water pooled in the sink with random drops swelling from the faucet and plopping in no discernable pattern.

When the winds gusted, the walls and the tin roof shook, the floorboards creaked, the chain of the central light rattled against the bulb, and the air pressure dropped. When from the south or west, the wind whistled through a series of cracks in the walls, a chorus of high-pitched tones that often sounded like off-key music.

Three children, each one chained to a metal post cemented into the floor, laid on the three beds, asleep or passed out or away in a mental happy place to avoid the truth of their situation, unimaginable for most people, dark and sinister. All were clothed in only underwear and tank-tops, grubby from head to toe with matted hair and dirt under their fingernails. The children did not belong there. They were captives, slaves, living and breathing toys for an unrelenting and tortured devil the likes of which people only believe exist in stories and nightmares. But sometimes those kinds of stories are true, and sometimes nightmares are real.

Day after day, their master would appear from the dark, turning the key and twisting the emerald knob. The children listened all day for those familiar sounds: the metallic click and the slow, squeaky revolution. Their dread reached a crescendo as the heavy booted footsteps fell on the noisy floorboards, the smell of sweat and diesel sweeping through the air as their captor entered and prepared himself for whatever special brand of torment he would force the innocent and terrified children to. Some days would involve nothing more than being offered food and water for which they were grateful to receive, but other days held unknown abuses for one or more of them.

Among those cruelties, they often went days without heat, fine for the daytime, but torturous on chilly nights. The children had no blankets to keep them warm, so they curled into fetal positions, trembling all night. If only they could have huddled together to stay warm, but their captor kept them separate, the act of a callous bastard.

Seventeen days had passed since their capture. In their minds, it easily could have been seventeen months. Time crawled forward, every minute an hour and every day endless. For the prior two days, the children had been denied food and water but also the presence of their master. As ghastly as it might sound, with their survival instincts kicking in, they secretly wished for him to arrive. The need for sustenance outweighed their desire for an escape from the physical abuses that were sure to come. They were whittling away. Their calorie intake was already dangerously low, but with two straight days and not so much as a glass of water, death sprinted toward them.

2

Thursday, November 8th, 2012 – 5:30 a.m.
Lansing, Michigan

Cole Redman awoke from a restless night's sleep even more exhausted then when he slumped into bed six hours earlier. The week leading up to that day every year was excruciating and tiresome. Not a day had gone by in twenty years that he didn't think about how fortunate he was to even be alive, but the emotional turmoil he endured because of a terrible choice he made as an eleven-year-old haunted him with belligerent vigor. He knew only one thing for sure - he was alive and they were dead.

For reasons unknown to Cole, this year's anniversary was particularly hard to face. He was in his early thirties now and had never been able to find real joy or peace in his life. He never married as he couldn't hold onto a girlfriend for longer than six months before the melancholy extended beyond his own soul and bled into the relationship. He was alone and had no real friends, and it had been that way for as long as he could remember. It came to define him.

Why so glum, his co-workers always asked. *You might be bi-polar Cole,* they suggested. *Happiness is a choice,* they might have said. *No,* Cole would think, *I simply made a horrible and selfish decision a long time ago, and now I have to live with the guilt of that. Maybe I just don't deserve to live,* he often contemplated.

His drive to McCarron & Webster, the accounting firm and only place Cole had been employed since graduating from college, offered nothing special. He lived only a short distance from the main office downtown, usually a twenty-five-minute drive in moderate traffic. He pulled through the drive-thru of his favorite local coffee shop for a Grande, sugar-free vanilla, whole milk latte, and always left the one dollar and four cent change from his five-dollar bill in the plastic tip container.

Once inside the underground parking structure of his company's twenty-seven story office building, he found his usual parking spot - two levels down with a large concrete pillar on the driver's side and three spaces away from the elevator. Getting in at 7 a.m. had its advantages, consistent parking and light traffic being two of them.

Cole trudged his way to the elevator, stood still and silent for the ride up to the 14th floor, and again trudged his way to the two-person cubicle he shared with fellow external auditor James Hagden. The two men were polar opposites in just about every way, though they got along just fine as co-workers. Cole, thirty-one years old, was six feet two inches tall with short cropped black hair, sapphire rich blue eyes, a little pasty, clean shaven, and held a quiet apathy on his face and in his body language.

James, contrarily, boiled with enthusiasm, smiled often, was only five feet eight inches tall and a little pudgy around the mid-section, with collar length, shaggy, speckled grey hair, beard, and moustache. Nearing fifty, he had been married for twenty-seven years and had three children, the oldest in college seeking a Master's degree in Education, the youngest a sophomore in high school.

Their floor of the building was typical for modern offices - gray carpet, gray walls, bright fluorescents mixed within drop ceiling panels, people walking about, phones ringing, computer keyboards clicking wildly, and indiscriminate voices floating through the air. The elevators opened to the middle of a long hallway with an off-shoot walkway to the left and the right. Down each walkway were dozens of openings to two-person cubicles with five-foot gray dividing walls.

"Morning, Cole," James greeted with a half wave and a full smile. "You all ready for the meeting this morning?" he asked after turning his attention back to his laptop where he typed aggressively.

"Almost. I gotta type up the summary real quick, but other than that, I'm done," Cole said as he slid his bag under the desk. He left his jacket on, a dark brown, lightweight, fully zipping polyester rain jacket. At work, he rarely took it off, something he used as an unconscious shield from penetrating personalities, or perhaps, more like a casing to hold in his own distress. Then again, maybe he was always a little chilly and it fit his disposition.

He promptly pulled his chair away to sit down and pried open his laptop before hitting the power button. All the while, he gripped the coffee cup in his left hand, sipping a little every thirty seconds to keep the caffeine supply flowing. He had already made up his mind that a second cup from the Breakfast Express Station down the hall would be necessary that morning. He had lost two to three hours of sleep each night for the past four nights, not to mention the hours he did sleep were restive and filled with nightmares.

Cole drank the last bit of coffee and immediately tossed it into the small trashcan to the left of his desk. Once his computer fully loaded, he logged in and brought up his email. He stared at the screen but didn't actually read anything, instead fighting his heavy eyelids. He reflexively reached for his paper cup but sighed loudly after grasping at the air.

"Everything okay? You're looking even more morose than usual my friend," James said, who at that point had gotten up and was standing right behind Cole.

"Tired. Haven't slept well in a few days. Lot on my mind I guess." Cole turned and jumped back in his chair upon finding James so close. "Jesus, Jim!"

"Sorry. I thought you sensed my presence."

"I'm just out of it." Cole reached to the key he wore on a silver chain around his neck, a constant reminder of his past, yet often a soothing one. He rubbed the cool steel between the thumb and index finger of his right hand and took a few deep breaths. "I need more coffee.

Wanna walk down to the station with me? You can remind me of the travel details of our upcoming trip to Ohio." Cole rose from his seat and reached for his back pocket to make sure he had money in his wallet. He was so tired he couldn't recall how many bills were left after his drive-thru purchase barely thirty minutes earlier. He was happy to discover forty-eight dollars.

"Sure. I could use a muffin or something." James stepped back to allow Cole the space to walk past him, then gave him a you first gesture. Cole took it and James quickly followed. Once they entered the main hall passage, James sped up and walked side by side with Cole. "You ever been to Dayton? I've traveled through there a couple of times myself but nothing major."

"No. Other than business trips, I've never really been anywhere."

When they reached the breakfast area, the stand with the daily newspaper caught Cole's eye. The title of the lead article, in particular, is what really drew his attention. It read: *Two local children still missing after exhaustive 72-hour search.* Cole stopped dead in his tracks and just stared at the newspaper. Instantly, he grew anxious, his heart rate buzzed upward, and the palms of his hands moistened with a clammy nervousness.

"Cole? You all right? You literally look like you've seen a ghost," James said. Cole offered no response. "Hey!" James shouted, trying to snap Cole from whatever spell he was under.

"What?" Cole asked as he jerked from his trance. He felt hot and wiped the sweat from his forehead and smeared it on his right pant leg. His pale skin had grown markedly more so. "I ... sorry. I don't feel very good right now." He swallowed hard.

"You don't look very good right now either."

"I think I need to go sit down." Cole turned to a small area near the food station with eight bistro-sized tables and stools. The first table was empty, so he took a seat with James cradling his right arm to prevent him from falling.

"Can I get you something? Maybe some hot tea?" James asked.

"No. I think I'm okay. Just got a little lightheaded for a second," Cole said. He took repeated deep breaths, bringing himself back to normal within a few moments.

"Just stay here for a bit. I'm going to go grab my muffin. How about a coffee?"

"Yeah, I'll take one. Thanks." Cole rubbed his hands together and looked around the room to try and clear his head. He always had good instincts for impending bad situations and this felt like one of those times, but with the significance of that particular day on his mind, anything else would need to take a backseat.

Clearly, his gut feelings were trying to tell him something but the emotional relapse he experienced upon seeing the newspaper would get lost in the shuffle of ghosts and enduring mistakes.

"Be right back then," James said. He left the seating area and headed back toward the food and drink line.

Cole zoned out for the four minutes it took James to return with his coffee. James placed the cup in front of Cole and took a seat across from him with his muffin and a plastic pint of 2% milk.

"What do I owe ya?" Cole asked.

"I got this one. You can get the next," James suggested. Cole nodded. James peeled the muffin paper away and tore the bottom off the muffin, placing the entire piece in his mouth. "Maybe you should go home?"

Cole shrugged his shoulders while wrapping his fingers around the lidless paper cup. He carefully sipped and found it scorching hot. He blew on the liquid a few times before taking any subsequent sips. The two men sat in silence while they ate and drank, James watching Cole to make sure he was improving.

"I've heard we are getting an early flu bug around here. With temps this month being colder than usual, people are getting sick sooner too.

Maybe you caught it?" James asked.

"I doubt it. I've got insomnia real bad right now and I think I just need to get some damn sleep. I'll be fine." Cole's tone turned abrupt with his last words, trying to end the conversation. With his right index finger and thumb, Cole rubbed his forehead as if he had a headache. He knew exactly why he wasn't feeling well, he just didn't care to discuss it. Tomorrow would be a new day, he knew that too, but first he had to pay his annual penance for the sins of his past. He didn't like it but he accepted it nonetheless. Guilt was his partner in life, one he couldn't divorce, one he couldn't kill, one that had become as much a part of his identity as his own name.

James accepted the signs and backed off from the chatter. He sat quietly and finished his muffin and milk while Cole took down half his coffee. Not another word was said during the break.

They left the table together, each throwing their trash in a can on the way out of the seating area. Cole made a point to keep the newspaper out of his eye line as he walked back to their cubicle.

At their desks, James quickly sat down and was immediately back to work, pecking away at the keys and fully immersed in an email conversion before Cole could even read through the first message from his inbox.

Cole decided to skip the emails, instead he brought up an empty document to begin typing up his case summary for the team's latest auditing project. The meeting at 9 a.m. was the deadline for the team to present the report. The clock in the corner of his monitor read 7:20 a.m. He took a full ninety minutes to complete the summary. He sent the file to the printer and ran off enough copies to pass around to the managers he assumed would attend the meeting.

As Cole got up from his chair to fetch the documents from the printer, the mail clerk, Karl, a twenty-two year old 70's throwback to pot smoking, corduroy wearing hippies, rolled up to the cubicle with his chrome cart. From the first of the three tan bins on the top shelf of the cart, Karl pulled a small bundle and handed it to James, who tossed it on his desk to deal with later. Karl then picked up a single six-inch by nine-inch manila envelope from the middle bin and offered it to Cole.

Cole received the mail and glanced at the front. A puzzled gaze drew across his face. He smirked at the odd nature of what was written on it in red Sharpie marker:
COLE REDMAN
5 ...
"Where did this come from?" Cole asked.
"No idea man. It was sitting with the rest of

the mail already sorted for the auditing department when I got in this morning. There's no postage, so I assume it's interoffice." Karl turned back to his cart and moved to the next area without another word.

"We gotta go, Cole. Meeting time," James said with wide eyes.

Cole shook his head to refocus his attention toward the meeting. He would have to deal with the odd envelope later. He stuffed it into the large pocket inside the right side of his jacket, intent on checking it out during a dull point of the meeting. Cole grabbed the documents and his laptop and followed James, who was ten steps ahead.

3

Thursday, November 8th, 2012 – 3:40 p.m.
Lansing, Michigan

Cole sat in his car after a long day at work. His morning meeting went well, though he sat mentally absent for most of it. Their team received confirmation and travel plans for the next audit job in Dayton, Ohio. At the end of the work day the following Tuesday, they would drive a company van to Dayton and stay in a hotel, not a great hotel, but not an awful one either, probably a Holiday Day Inn Express. From Wednesday through Friday, they would do their usual business of inspecting and reconciling the financials of the company that had hired them.

Cole would buy coffee somewhere instead of drinking the free hotel crap each morning. His per diem would easily cover the cost. He ate cheap, but in most cases, he preferred coffee to food. James did the opposite. He took full advantage of the continental breakfast, ate a small lunch, then blew his entire per diem on a large dinner. *If they're going to offer it, I might as well use it,* James would say. Cole didn't give a hoot either way.

When he finally got the nerve up to start the car, he pulled out of his spot and made his way north on Stoney Drive. He had a stop to make before heading home, the same one he made every year on that day, one he lamented but never missed, not even once.

The sun burned through the driver's side window, low on the horizon with two hours left of daylight. Despite this, the glass was cool to the touch with the air temperature in the low thirties.

By the time he would get home, darkness would prevail. Cole hated getting home after dark. The evening always felt too short. One of the big upsides to his current job was getting off at 3:30 p.m., because even in the midst of winter, it came with an hour of light, which wasn't much, but it was enough to keep him sane. With

December fast approaching, each day brought one less minute of daylight, and for Cole, one more minute of misery.

After a thirty-five minute drive to the north edge of town, Cole pulled up to the wrought iron gate of a heavily tree-lined property. No one attended the gate, as people were free to come and go as they pleased, but it was shut and locked promptly at eight in the evening and reopened each day at six in the morning.

The cemetery was well kept with mostly newer tombstones and small statues in straight rows. Built in 1987, Cole had witnessed the gradual spread of grave markers from the west and east edges, working their way toward the center road and now 90% full.

Cole drove his late model, two-door, navy blue sedan slow, like he was sneaking up on someone, or maybe he was just in no rush to get to his destination. About one hundred feet from where he intended to stop, he drove partially in the grass to get around a silver conversion van, older and rusty with bald tires, parked with no regard to other traffic.

"Asshole," Cole said as he glanced back to catch a view of the front of the van. There was no one in sight. He turned back to the road and continued on, pulling off to the right before coming to a stop in his usual spot. He imagined a sign marking the location he always parked that read: Chicken Shits Stop Here.

He locked his gaze forward for a few moments, staring at nothing, gathering the courage to once again face his past and wonder why the Universe saw fit to keep him around yet take the others. He acknowledged there could be other forces at work but he could not deny his own responsibility, and what, if anything, would have been different had he made other choices.

He turned the key and pulled it from the ignition after putting the car in park. He jammed the keys into his left, front pants pocket and turned to the passenger seat where a small potted plant sat with a white plastic bag covering the foliage. Cole gently pulled the bag from the plant and tossed it aside. The plant, a Red Trillium, sometimes called a Three-leaf Nightshade, had moderately sized green leaves, each cluster sprouting three tender, purplish-red flowers bursting from the center. He grew the plant at home indoors ever since he had first discovered it.

While walking through a local hardware store with his mother the summer after 'the incident', the beautiful potted plant caught Cole's attention, with the mysterious and haunting three-leaved blossoms. The three ... the three ... the three ... speaking to him like ghosts from his recent past.

He begged his mom to get it for him, something to take care of, to nurture, for Cole to use as a symbol of his ordeal, one only he knew the full details of. She did, and now for the twentieth time, he would pluck one flower from the plant and take it with him to the graves.

Slowly, he opened his car door and exited the vehicle, each move deliberate and forced. He awkwardly zipped his jacket all the way up while trying not to crush the delicate petals of his most and least favorite flower, if such a thing is possible.

In the far north-west edge of the cemetery, a weeping willow cascaded wide and low over a large area containing two grave markers about ten feet from the base of the tree. Cole brushed aside one branch and stepped into the thinning canopy. The graves were side by side and five feet apart. Each was marked with the same style tombstone, two and a half feet tall and two feet in width, simple brown stone, tiny crosses on the face near the top, the text just below that.

Cole stood centered in front of the two markers, his head down and eyes closed. He caressed the key resting on his chest, as he often did. He was not a man of prayer, so he spoke directly to them, hoping somewhere in the ether they could hear him.

"There is nothing I can say that I haven't

already said. I failed you both and for that I am eternally sorry." Cole took a deep breath, no less nervous and saddened on that day of memorial than the first. "I often think about the kind of people you both would've become were you still around. I know we barely knew each other, but I do my best with the little information I have about you both. We spent seventeen days together, a lifetime if you ask me, and though you two were actual siblings, I feel very much like your older brother. But I failed in that responsibility. I let my own fear and cowardice guide my actions. I hid ... hell, I still hide from the truth, but not a day goes by that I don't regret, that I don't ... wish, I could have taken your places."

The rustling of leaves and branches nearby broke Cole from his words, drawing his attention to the left. Looking over in the direction of the noise, he saw nothing.

"Hello?" No one answered. Cole ducked his head down to look beneath the willow's branches and again saw nothing. He brushed it off as the sounds of nature and went back to his reason for being there.

He held the flower in his right hand and stepped toward the left tombstone. He plucked one of the three petals from the Red Trillium and placed it on the ground, nestling it to the base of the stone. "'Lil Kylie, with the big blue eyes, I hope you forgive me and are resting peacefully." A stream of tears rolled from the corner of Cole's left eye.

He turned his attention to the right, stepping over to face the other marker. He again plucked a petal from the flower, repeating the placement. "Justin, my adopted brother, I'm sorry." Cole stopped and looked up to the willow tree and sighed deep before looking back down. "I'm so, so sorry. I was an unbelievable bastard, selfish, and a big chicken shit. You both deserved better and I deserve nothing. I hope you forgive me."

Wasting no time and ready to go home, Cole finished his ritual by taking the final petal and inserting it into his mouth, gently placing it on his tongue, much like the body of Christ wafer in Catholic communion. He let the tart and bitter penetrate his glands before chewing and swallowing, a minor torture he deemed necessary.

Once the foliage slid down, he turned and walked back to his car, still sobbing, exhausted, and all set for an early bedtime. As he opened the door, he remembered the van and glanced over to find it no longer there. "Asshole," Cole repeated for no other reason than to help relieve his own stress. He entered his car, returned the plastic bag to the plant, and left the cemetery in a better mood, though barely detectable on the surface.

4

Sunday, November 8th, 1992 – 2:08 a.m.
Rural Ingham County, Michigan

Metal on metal scraped. A loud click followed by a high-pitched squeak from the emerald knob turning awoke the children from a light sleep. The time of day was unknown to them. They slumbered nearly all of the previous forty-eight hours, mostly because they lacked the energy to do anything else. They needed food or they might not make it another two days, so the children were cautiously optimistic about the man's return. His presence, at least, meant a small chance they would get to eat.

He entered the room as if there was nothing going on, as if the children were not there. Only shadow followed him, the predawn hours black with a haze of soft, gray moonlight. He slammed the door open and again slammed it behind him. He turned back to the door and used a key to lock it from the inside. Even though the children were chained to their beds, he wouldn't risk one of them escaping, so he always made sure the door remained locked at all times.

The three children – eight-year-old Kylie, her older brother - ten-year-old Justin, and their schoolmate, eleven-year-old Cole, didn't move as the man entered but they sure watched him. The man made no eye contact with the children; instead, he walked with heavy steps to the sink, dropping a large set of keys and the single cabin key on its own ring on the table as he went by. He didn't like the idea of carrying the cabin key around with him all the time, so when he got home, it hung on a hook of its own, separate and isolated from the others, much like he viewed the cabin and his life away from it.

With the arm at his side, he carried something in his right hand that hung down almost to the floor. He tossed the item into the sink near the left side, shifted the faucet to the right, and turned the cold knob. He filled the three plastic cups that sat on the edge of the sink with water, turned off the faucet, and carried them to the table.

One at a time, he brought a cup to each child. He watched each one drink the whole thing down before going back to grab another to give to the next child. He started with Kylie. She was so weak she could barely hold the cup, almost dropping it three times.

The man was not thrilled about her pace. "Drink it," he muttered with a grainy, deep voice. A minute went by and he grew impatient. "Drink it, drink it, drink it," he repeated with accelerating intensity.

Kylie took a full two minutes to get her water down but was relieved to get it. His urging to speed up did not phase her one bit. After the horror she had already endured, his voice became idol against her emergent courage.

The man snatched the cup from her, placing it on the table before grabbing the next. Justin and Cole each took less than thirty seconds to down their waters. They were old enough to recognize the man was harder on them than on Kylie, and he would draw his hand quicker when they stepped out of line.

After seventeen days, the fight inside of them had slowly turned from feisty to cooperative. They hoped to appeal to some part of the man that was still human, still compassionate, but the man held no empathy, no heart. Any evidence that might suggest he had feelings was nothing more than a means to an end for him, a cause and effect situation. If the man thought it served him in some way, he would do it. If the action or words would not serve his purposes, they would be dismissed or would never exist to begin with.

The children did the best they could, their own survival instincts at work, but they did not know the man, his history, his mind, or the dark and empty places within his psyche.

The man picked up the large set of keys from the table and turned his attention back to the children, hovering over them like a storm cloud frozen in time. They kept their heads down and bodies perfectly still, not wanting to invite his attention. No matter what happened, one of them would be chosen, one of them would lose a little more of their soul.

In a moment of impatience, Cole lifted his head from his knees ever so slightly, drawing the attention of their captor, who promptly stepped around to the side of Cole's mattress to unlock his cuff. The child's stomach soured and his hands shook. If he had anything but water in his belly, he would have vomited, but he held it together.

The devil grabbed Cole's wrist and lifted him from the mattress and onto the floor, pushing him to walk away from the beds and toward the table.

"Go to the sink and eat," the man commanded. "Pick off what you want and eat it right there ... but leave some for the others." The man released Cole's arm and shoved him forward. Cole stumbled but kept his feet beneath him as he walked to the sink.

The light was too dim to see clearly what food awaited him. With a timid vacillation, Cole lowered his left hand into the sink to discover something relatively smooth but somewhat spongy. He moved his hand up and down the length of his meal, about two feet long, maybe four inches wide. When he got to one end and his fingers made contact with the fur from the tail of the squirrel, he jerked his hand back. Cole knew immediately what he was dealing with. Their captor had caught the animal in a trap outside, chopped off the head, let it bleed out, skinned it, with the exception of the tail (something to carry it by), pierced it with a rod, and cooked it over a fire pit. Several hours later, when it was convenient for him, the man arrived at the cabin.

"Tear at it with your fingers kid," the man suggested. "It won't bite you. It's either that or you starve," he added as he tossed the keys back on the table. He then disappeared behind the bamboo room divider where the siblings waited anxiously for their turn to eat.

With the index and middle finger of his left hand, Cole dove in, piercing the charred exterior of the animal flesh, using his thumb to grab and tear away a piece. He placed the tip of the meat just past his lips to taste it with his tongue, and after finding it rather appealing in texture and taste, inserted the rest. Cole chewed just a few times before swallowing and dove in for another piece. So focused on the food, he lost track of the whereabouts of the man and what he might be doing.

Unconsciously, Cole heard things being said by the man: *take off ... underwear / flip ... hands and knees, boy / if you cry ... I'll put ... her / shut up!* He also heard whimpering from Justin and the gentle crying of Kylie while her brother was assaulted. Cole did not flinch at the sounds and words while he ate but ideas swirled in his head, thoughts about a life away from the torture, and an apparent lapse in the attention to detail normally exhibited by their devil.

Cole ate seven bites of meat, but to make sure Kylie and Justin would have enough, he stopped short of satiety. He quietly turned on the cold-water faucet and used his cupped hands to drink a little more water and rinse off his fingertips. After shutting off the water, he turned to face the table. The realization of Justin's torture finally came to light for him. He shook his head in disbelief of the situation, trying desperately to shift his focus. He longed for the arms of his mother surrounding him, his warm and safe bed, a simple bowl of chicken noodle soup and a grilled cheese sandwich made with Velveeta. He closed his eyes and became lost for a moment in those wonderful thoughts. Cole came back to reality as a gust of wind hit the cabin, forcing chilly air through the room and sending goose pimples across his entire body.

When he opened his eyes, the key sitting on the table called to him. The idea of grabbing it and escaping had already crossed his mind while he ate but he had quickly dismissed the idea as too risky, for if he failed, the man would relentlessly beat him as punishment. In the two-plus weeks since they were kidnapped, there had been no better opportunity, so it lingered in Cole's mind as he stood there, refusing to relent.

With light feet, Cole stepped to the table to take a closer look. The unusual key stood out, befitting the unique door of the cabin.

Cole pondered the sequence of events that would need to take place, leading to his freedom. *Grab the key, sneak to the door and unlock it, run like hell and don't stop until I find help.* As the words rolled through his mind, the confidence to act grew strong. *What will he do to me if I try and fail? Then again, what will he do to me if I stay and do nothing?*

If he was going to make a break for it, the time had come. Weak, scared, and weary of the hell they were enduring, Cole drew on every ounce of courage he could muster and put his plan into motion.

He stepped forward and put two fingers on the key. As slow as he could after pinching the key between his fingers, Cole drew his hand upward, watching the ring rise and leave the table. There was no sound, and not just from the table, but from behind the bamboo divider as well. *Oh no!*

Cole felt he had nothing to lose, so he abandoned his stealth and bolted for the door with the key out in front of his body like a guiding force. He scratched around the keyhole until the key entered. He turned it twice to the left until he heard the click, hands trembling.

Their captor reacted to the commotion and surfaced from the bed area with a scowl. "You little shit," he scorned. "You just made a big, big mistake."

Cole pulled the key from the lock and turned his head to face the devil. The fire in the man's eyes said everything. Without a word, Cole turned back to the door, twisted the emerald knob, and pulled the door halfway open.

The man quickly stepped forward to snatch Cole, figuring the kid would freeze in fear. The man was wrong.

Cole disappeared through the opening, and with all the strength and energy he had left, ran and ran and ran. The sky was gray-smothered black, the nearly full moon providing the only light but the perfect amount to allow Cole to run in the dark yet still see his way through the forest of oak and birch and maple. The leaves and twigs crunched beneath his every step and tore at his feet, although they were too cold and numb for him to know the damage.

At first, he ran as straight as his hobbled steps could, but eventually, he began darting in different directions to avert his pursuer. He never once looked back, and thus, had no way of knowing he had lost his captor after just four minutes. Cole ran for another twelve minutes, until his feet bled, his lungs feeling like they could no longer take in air, his heart racing, and the muscles in his legs no longer able to bear his weight.

When he reached the asphalt edge of a road in the middle of nowhere, Cole collapsed in the rocky soil just off the side of that county road, unconscious.

A few hours later, just as the sun was breaking

the horizon, a silver minivan slammed to a stop when the driver noticed his body on the side of the road - bloodied, bruised, filthy, and wearing nothing but grungy briefs and a torn tank-top.

A woman exited the van and ran to the boy. She knelt down beside him and spoke. "Oh my god! Are you okay?" She reached for the boy's wrist to check for a pulse. Faint, but there.

In a fog, Cole tried to open his eyes when he heard the voice and warm touch of the woman. "Mom?" he muttered before passing out again.

"Oh ... thank god you're alive. Just stay still. I'll call 9-1-1," the woman said. She ran back to her vehicle, pulled her newly acquired Nokia cell phone from her purse, and dialed emergency. Later, she would comment over and over again about how awesome it was to have a portable phone, if for no other reason than getting roadside help.

She explained to the operator how she found a young boy on the side of the road, without clothes, emaciated, dirty, and nearly unconscious. Help was on the way.

She returned to Cole. "Everything is going to be okay. I called for help." Another vehicle pulled up behind the woman's van to offer assistance.

Three minutes later, two police cruisers and an ambulance charged onto the scene and took control of the situation.

***

Cole awoke to the bright overhead light of a hospital room. His mother, Gretchen, had not left the room since she arrived at his bedside, and when she saw his eyes open, she jumped from her chair to hold his hand and welcome him back.

"Cole, baby. How are you feeling?" Gretchen asked as she gently rubbed his cheek.

"Mom?"

"Yes baby, I'm here ... and you're safe. You in any pain?"

Cole's vision fully returned after waking from the deepest sleep he had ever experienced. He would never be more physically and emotionally exhausted.

"Mom ... I really, really want a piece of pizza. I'm so hungry."

Gretchen could not help but laugh a little with a big grin on her face. "Oh, Cole. I'll get you whatever you want. You've been through a heck of an ordeal and I'm just glad to have you back. Everyone thought you were gone forever but I knew you'd be back. A mother knows. I knew baby." She planted a gentle kiss on his cheek. "I'll be right back. See what I can do about getting you some pizza."

Just as she started to walk away, Cole leaned forward and grabbed her arm. "Don't leave me. I don't want to be alone. Don't leave me," Cole begged. He released her arm and slumped back to his pillow, breathing heavy, plum out of energy.

"I'll be right out in the hall and only for a second, so I'll be back in a jiffy," Gretchen said. She patted Cole's arm before leaving with hurried steps, anxious to get back to her son. Twenty second later, Cole was asleep again.

5

Friday, November 9th, 2012 – 5:30 a.m.
Lansing, Michigan

Cole slept deep but his mind ran hard with dreams of his past. As he shuffled the blanket off his body, he wondered how many more times he could suffer the failures of his childhood. Sitting with feet hanging over the edge of the bed, he rubbed the sleep from his eyes with the middle finger from each hand. His stomach refused to allow him food the day before, so he woke up starving.

Ten minutes in a hot shower brought him to life, at least as much as could be expected without his coffee. He got dressed for work and went straight to the kitchen to scrounge around for a rare weekday breakfast. Most days, coffee was it for mornings, but occasionally on the weekends, Cole enjoyed a bowl of cold cereal.

Before bothering to bring out a bowl and the cereal box, he opened the fridge to check for unspoiled milk. He was in luck. The half-gallon he had bought the previous Friday was mostly full, and the expiration date and a quick smell test satisfied him enough to continue his pursuit.

Cole took the first spoonful slow and enjoyed it thoroughly. The subsequent bites were not so controlled. He wolfed the rest down in less time than it took to prep the bowl. When he finished, he got up from the table, threw his bowl and spoon in the sink, and stood there for a moment. His stomach rumbled with uneasy bubbling. A sudden urge to vomit overcame him, and before he could even think to run to the bathroom, his breakfast came back up right into the sink. Two surges were all that was needed to empty his stomach.

He turned on the cold water, rinsed out the sink, and his mouth, then drank a little water from the tap.

Cole needed some rest after a tough week and little to no sleep, and with the big meeting at work done, he knew his work schedule for the day would be light. This prompted a decision to call in sick. Using his cell phone, he placed the call to his boss, then sent an email to his team to let them know personally he would not be in. There was no issue from anyone on him taking a sick day. The team had seen the signs of distress emanating from Cole the whole week. James, his cubicle-mate and the closet thing he had to a friend, saw firsthand Thursday morning how bad it was getting, and via a reply email, asked Cole to get some extra rest over the weekend, and if he could, find something fun to do. Even through his barriers, Cole felt the warmth and friendship coming from James and accepted a little in, certainly more than he normally would. There's nothing more likely to demonstrate a human being's need for the caring of other people than being sick, even for Cole. He missed his mother at times like that.

Too ill for coffee, Cole forced himself back to bed where he slept for another three hours. When he awoke for the second time that day, his stomach felt better, so he decided to go for a walk to pick up a coffee from an independent coffee shop a few blocks from his house.

At the entry table and coat rack by his front door, he slipped on his jacket, picked his wallet up from the table and slid it in his back-left pants pocket, and stuffed his keys in the front right pants pocket. Once outside, he shut the door with only the handle locked, leaving the deadbolt free. He wouldn't be gone long, so he wasn't too worried about someone breaking in. *What would they steal? I don't have anything.*

With those thoughts, he zipped his jacket all the way up and inhaled the crisp air of a Midwestern early November morning. He blew the moist air from his lungs and watched it freeze as it escaped his mouth, pretending he was blowing smoke just like he had done since he was young and first discovered the phenomenon.

Immediately, Cole regretted not wearing gloves but he knew the coffee cup would keep his hands warm on the walk back, Besides, the sun was shining and would only get brighter as the morning went on.

Cole kept his head tilted down toward the sidewalk as he walked, looking up every few seconds to make sure he could anticipate obstacles. About a block from his house, he got a strange feeling, like someone was breathing on the back of his neck. He shivered and turned to look back but continued walking. About one hundred twenty feet down the road, a silver van, much like the one he encountered at the cemetery, crept along like molten lava on a gradual slope. Cole didn't think much of it at first, so he turned forward and kept walking.

A light bulb grew bright in his mind as he remembered where he had seen the van before. "That can't be a coincidence. Maybe the guy heard me call him an asshole and he wants to give me a piece of his mind. Oops," he said, playfully. Cole glanced back to find the van still there and still going forward, fifty feet closer than just a few seconds earlier. Cole's pace quickened. He was in no mood to have a face-to-face confrontation with some overly sensitive quack.

His heart skipped a beat after hearing the engine of the van rev. When Cole looked back again, the van was close enough for him to see the driver's face. They made brief eye contact, though the driver had on sunglasses and a hoodie. The van sped off, rounding the corner ahead of Cole and disappearing down the road.

Cole stood there to calm down. He didn't like the feeling he was getting about that van. "What is that guy's problem? Geesh!" He reached to his left-front pants pocket for his phone so he could check his email, only to find nothing. He patted the rest of his pockets and his jacket when it dawned on him that he left his phone in the kitchen. Normally, he would leave it on the entry table so it would be easy to grab on the way out each day, but calling in sick took him out of his routine and it didn't even occur to him that something was missing when he left the house.

"I better go home and grab it, just in case." Cole jogged back home, telling himself he was just trying to stay warm, which may have been true to some degree, but he was nervous about the van too. He definitely didn't want to get caught in a situation without having his phone.

As he approached his front door, he noticed something odd. Taped to the center of the door and right at eye level was a photocopy of a newspaper article. The headline read: Missing Local Boy Found Alive. Cole read the words in stunned silence. The article started: An eleven-year-old local boy, Cole Redman, missing for seventeen days, was found alive on the side of a county road in rural Ingham County, east of Lansing. The sheriff's department has offered no information as to his prior whereabouts or the circumstances surrounding his disappearance...

Cole stopped himself from reading on. He tore the paper from the door and crumpled it in disgust, fear and anger swelling inside. *This is a sick prank. When I find out who's doing this, there will be hell to pay, you fuckers.* He looked down to the wad of paper in his hand and let out a deep sigh. Before his next thought could even coalesce, a sudden sharp pain radiated through his skull and everything went black.

6

Sunday, November 8th, 1992 – 11:02 a.m.
East Lansing, Michigan

A joint task force had been formed when Cole
was discovered on the side of the road. With a
child found in a rural area of the county, the
jurisdiction clearly fell to the local sheriff's
department, however, with multiple children
missing and all of them from the Lansing area,
that police department was handed the case. The
sheriff's department was simply not equipped to
handle a potential serial child kidnapping case,
nor did they have the manpower necessary to
launch a full investigation. The F.B.I. had their

hands in as well, but until it officially became a murder investigation, they let the locals handle it.

The lead detective, Todd Jebsen of the Lansing Municipal Police Department, took charge of the case right away. His first step in the investigation was to question Cole. A child advocate from the department came along to protect Cole, as the law required. The two officials met in the parking lot of St. Mary's Medical Center on the east side of town, entering the hospital together heading straight to room 332.

The boy was asleep. His mother sat next to him just watching his peaceful face as he dreamt, she hoped of pleasant things.

"Hello, Ms. Redman," Detective Jebsen greeted.

Gretchen turned her head. "Hello." They had already met when Gretchen filed a missing person's report upon Cole's disappearance and they had several phone conversations since.

"This is Dr. Emma Weinstein, child advocate."

"Nice to meet you," Gretchen said. She turned back to watching her son sleep.

"Ma'am, it's critical we question your son right now. Any details about where he's been and who he's been with are going to be as fresh in his mind right now as they ever will be," Detective Jebsen pleaded. He had a face and demeanor that allowed most people to instantly trust him but Gretchen was too focused on keeping her son safe and coddled after his seventeen-day absence. She did not warm up to him as quickly as most.

Without looking the detective in the face and just staring at the still sleeping Cole, Gretchen said, "I do appreciate that fact detective, but it hasn't even been a full day since I got my baby boy back. The thought of trying to pry information out of him seems cruel. We don't know what he's been through." She softly caressed Cole's hand, lightly shaking her head as she tried not to imagine the horrific details he may have endured. She also toiled with the truth of Detective Jebsen's words. If they were going to have a decent chance of finding who was responsible for Cole's abduction, time was their worst enemy.

"Let me assure you, Ms. Redman, we'll take great care in making Cole as comfortable as is possible, especially under the circumstances." Detective Jebsen placed his hand on her shoulder. "We need to catch the bastard who did this to your boy, and the only way that can happen is if we get some information from him. You do want to see justice done? We need your help here." He paused for a moment. "And unfortunately, you will not be allowed in the room when we question him, that's the law in cases like this, so we'll have to have you step out for a few minutes. But, that's why Dr. Weinstein is here, to be an advocate for Cole. She happens to be a child psychologist and a damn good one, which could be valuable in a case like this. She'll look out for his well-being."

Gretchen was not thrilled about the idea. "And you're absolutely sure I can't be here when you talk to him? He'll be so scared if I leave." Gretchen's eyes welled up as she spoke.

"I'm terribly sorry but no. Parents, when present, have a powerful influence on what their children will say. We'll need him to be as forthcoming as possible and he won't likely do that with you in the room. Again, I'm sorry, but that's just how it has to be. I hope you understand."

Gretchen quietly wept. After a few seconds of contemplation, she gathered some inner strength and rose from her bedside chair. She turned to Detective Jebsen and finally made eye contact. Without being able to pinpoint why, she felt safer after looking at him. His eyes held an unmistakable sincerity and an unexplainable trustworthiness, not on the surface really, but from somewhere in his soul.

She nodded, and without another word left the room, passing Dr. Emma Weinstein and a uniformed officer that manned the room from outside the door.

Detective Jebsen called Dr. Weinstein over to the bed where Cole was finally waking up after a long nap. No amount of sleep seemed like enough for him to catch up. He stayed awake for only short periods of time, generally less than thirty minutes before dozing back off, sometimes in mid conversation with his mother.

With the two adult strangers hovering over him, Cole opened his eyes expecting to see his mother or maybe a doctor or a nurse. Their presence confused him, causing his heart rate to increase with the growing anxiety. Even at his age, Cole understood that at some point he was going to have to face the authorities and answer some questions. He had only hoped it wouldn't be so soon.

"Hello, Cole. I'm Detective Jebsen but you can call me Jeb, all my friends do. This is Dr. Weinstein. She's here to make sure I treat you fairly, since you're a minor. I need to ask you some questions about your ordeal. You feel up to that?"

"Where's my mom? I really need my mom," Cole responded with indifference to the detective's inquiry.

"She's waiting outside. She'll be back shortly but right now we need to discuss what happened to you. Unfortunately, she can't be here while we do that."

"I don't feel very good. I need to see my mom."

"I'll be right back," Dr. Weinstein said. She exited the room and came back fifteen seconds later with Gretchen in tow. "Ma'am, if you could please tell your son how important this is."

Gretchen went around to the other side of the bed opposite the detective. Cole's eyes were heavy with doubts. She held his hand to offer reassurance as she spoke. "Cole, these people need to ask you some questions and you need to answer them as best you can."

"I don't feel very good. Can't we wait for a while?" Cole did his best to sound pitiful. His stomach churned with nervousness, so he wasn't lying, not entirely.

"No!" Gretchen barked. "We can't wait," Gretchen softened her tone. "It needs to be done now. Just think, if you get it done and over with now, you won't have to worry about it anymore. They need your memories to be as fresh as possible or something might get missed. You understand?"

He nodded but didn't like it. The truth was, he was scared to death to face any aspect of his nightmare. The thought of having to confront or even see the face of that devil again or be anywhere near that cabin, terrified him so much he'd probably never actually tell the whole truth, just to protect himself. The only x-factor for Cole was Justin and Kylie.

"I'll be right outside the room. This lady right here," Gretchen pointed her right hand toward Dr. Weinstein, "will make sure the police act appropriately, so don't hesitate to call on her if you feel uncomfortable. She's a doctor, so, she can help you deal with whatever feelings you might be having while you answer questions." Gretchen smiled. "Don't be afraid baby. Just be honest and tell them whatever you can remember. It'll be over before you know it."

She patted his arm, nodded, and left the room again, worried for her son but feeling better about the police. She just wanted to get through the tough stuff as quickly as possible so they could get on with their lives. This was a big first step. She wouldn't admit it at the time but she was as curious as anyone about the details of Cole's ordeal. Until then, she did not allow herself to dwell on the possibilities, but she knew, eventually, the details would emerge and they would have to deal with it, like the many challenges they would encounter.

To make Cole feel more comfortable, Detective Jebsen dragged the nearest chair up to the bedside and took a seat. He pulled a small, spiral notepad from his inside suit coat pocket and removed the blue ballpoint pen from the wire binding.

"We'll try to make this as quick and painless as possible. Okay?" The detective flipped his notepad to an empty page.

Cole nodded. Doubt and fear ran deep in his eyes, evident to both Dr. Weinstein and Detective Jebsen. Clearly, they would have to tread lightly or Cole was going to shut down before they got anything useful out of him.

"You've been missing for seventeen days, Cole. Do you remember what happened on the day you went missing?"

Cole shrugged his shoulders.

"Here ... let me be more specific. Did someone take you into their car and take you somewhere?" Jeb's voice was soothing and instantly made Cole feel safe. That comfort level gave Cole pause. He fully intended to hide the details of his abduction, but now he was having second thoughts.

Maybe I can trust him. They won't let ... him ... hurt me again. Cole closed his eyes for a moment. *No, no, no, no! The man is going to hurt me and hurt them. Never again. Never again.* He opened his eyes.

"I remember walking home from school, and then ... I was in a dark place." Cole stopped so he could carefully form the words. He didn't want to reveal too many details. He gently bit his lower lip. "I couldn't really see or hear anything. I ... I was dizzy a lot."

"That's good, Cole. Did you ever see another person? Like a man or a woman?" Jeb asked as he wrote down the boy's words. "You were gone for a long time."

"It didn't seem very long," Cole said. *It felt like forever.*

An image of the devil popped into Cole's mind, forcing him to shudder, his heart rate to shoot up, and his brow to sweat. Cole's body language was not lost on the doctor or the detective. They continued to pay close attention.

"I ... I don't really remember. There might have been ... a man. But I never saw his face," Cole quickly added.

"Do you remember anything at all about the place you were at? Was it a house, maybe in a basement? Any detail, even the smallest one, like colors, sounds, smells. They could all be important."

Cole just shook his head.

"Are you sure? Even the teensy, tiniest detail could help us figure out where you were?" From the pocket he had removed his notebook from, Jeb pulled an old, steel skeleton key on a ring and held it up to Cole. "This was in your hand when you were found you on the side of the road. Where did it come from?"

The sight of the key and the idea of the police

finding the cabin made Cole sick to his stomach. He quickly devised a lie to cover. "I found it on the playground at school a while back. I thought it was cool, so I kept it." He shook his head again. "But I'm sorry, I don't remember anything else."

Detective Jebsen could not determine whether Cole was telling the truth about the key. "That's perfectly all right. You're doing great," Jeb said with a firm reassurance. He handed the key to Cole who gripped it tight in his hand. "So, do you recall how you came to be on the side of the road this morning?"

Again, Cole thought hard about what he was going to reveal, and after repeating the words in his head a few times, he shared the information. "I woke up and I was laying on the floor." *Liar.* "It was too dark to see much, but when I looked around, I saw a little light coming from the corner and I could tell there was an open door." *Liar liar pants on fire.* Cole swallowed deep and his hands shook a little as he continued.

Dr. Weinstein kept a close eye on him, analyzing his words, his emotions, his tone. So far, she had not detected anything unusual.

"I just jumped up and decided to run away. I was dizzy at first, like my head was spinning around and around, but I made my way out of the door and just kept running until my legs hurt so bad I just stopped and fell down. I can't really remember what happened after that." Cole's lower lip quivered as he unsuccessfully fought back his tears. "I just ... woke up here," he finished through his sobbing.

"It's okay, Cole. Take a minute." Detective Jebsen pulled two tissues from the box on the table next to Cole's bed and handed them over. "I know this has been tough on you, but you're safe now, back with your mom." The detective looked to Dr. Weinstein and directed her to the other side of the room for a private chat.

"We're going to talk for a minute over there. We'll be back in just a second. We're almost done, so hang in there buddy."

Cole dabbed the edges of his eyes and his cheeks, then nodded. He blew his nose as the other two stepped over near the door.

"He's holding back a little, which is perfectly normal. At his age, it's common for the child to be fearful that the assailant who hurt them is too strong and powerful and will also hurt the people trying to help ... if he's found," Dr. Weinstein said.

"That makes sense. If you think he's holding back something, any suggestions as to how I can get more from him?" Jeb asked. "I was about to ask him if there were other children there and if he knows Justin and Kylie Simpson. They all go to the same school but are different ages and in different classes. His mother doesn't think he knows them."

"Well, maybe if you had a story you could tell him that might bring to light your strength as a police officer, so he feels more comfortable with the idea that if he gives you details about the assailant, you could take him down with no problem. Anything like that come to mind?"

"Hmmm." The detective scratched the back of his head. "Well, I've had plenty of interesting arrests, especially from when I was in vice, but nothing so flashy as you might see on NYPD Blue. I could embellish a little."

"Doesn't have to be the truth, but don't make it too sensational or he might not believe you. Just focus on your toughness and your special abilities as a cop. We need him to feel safe, like no matter what happens, you'll be able to protect him."

"Okay. I'll give it try. Thanks." Detective Jebsen sighed and shook his head. "Abductions are just terrible, but when it's kids, it's just ... mind-boggling."

"Yes it is."

They made their way back to Cole, the doctor returning to the end of the bed and the detective back to the chair.

Jeb took a deep breath. "Okay, Cole. We're

almost done." He flipped back through his notepad to find some information. "You go to Washington Grade School, right?"

"Yes." Cole rubbed a little moisture from the corner of his right eye and sniffed.

"You wouldn't happen to know a Justin or Kylie Simpson? They are a brother and sister that go to your school. They're younger than you though."

Cole tried hard to hide his surprise at the mention of the names of his fellow captives. He had barely been conscious long enough since his escape to even think about them, but the detective saying their names brought back a flood of memories. The change in Cole's demeanor and his watery eyes were evident.

"You okay, Cole?" Jeb asked with a concerned tone.

Cole nodded then cleared his throat. "Yes. Sorry. I'm really tired." He shook his head. "I don't know them. They go to my school?"

"Yes they do. You sure you don't know them?"

"Pretty sure. Why? Who are they?" *Oh god. What I am doing?*

"It doesn't matter." Detective Jebsen quickly changed the subject. "I'd like to tell you a quick story about this really mean and very, very bad guy the police were looking for a few years ago."

He saw Cole's eyes perk up a little, so he knew he at least had the boy's curiosity. "I won't get into the details of all the bad things this criminal did, but let's just say, he hurt a lot of people ... and even killed a few."

"Why? Why did he hurt people? Did you arrest him?"

"There is no easy answer to the question of why bad people do what they do. This guy had a really rough childhood and he never got the help he needed from his parents or people like me." Jeb motioned to Dr. Weinstein. "Or like the doctor, someone who could help him sort out all the bad things that happened to him when he was younger. Does that make sense?"

"I think so," Cole responded.

"So, yes, we did arrest him but it took a lot of hard work. The biggest factor was the help we got from one of the people that he hurt. They gave valuable information about what he looked like, where he was staying, etc." Detective Jebsen paused for a minute to evaluate Cole's demeanor, which in that moment didn't reveal much. "Of course, once we found him in the abandoned warehouse down on the riverfront, he was not going to go down without a fight."

"What happened?" Cole asked as he gently rocked back and forth, anxious to hear more of the story.

"Well, when we arrived on the scene, he had barricaded himself inside a room with three hostages and he was threatening to hurt them if we didn't leave. But there was no way we were leaving," Jeb said as he shook his head vigorously. He then took a few moments to carefully choose his next words. "That's not what we do. We save people from guys like him. We DO NOT ... back down." Jeb threw a glance at Dr. Weinstein, who gave a subtle nod.

"So, we sent officers into the building and they pinned him in a room where it appeared that he had no way out. The thing was, I had a feeling this guy was a little smarter than we were giving him credit for, so I decided to take an officer with me and head around to an alley behind the building to cover a rear entrance. Turns out I was right. As soon as he caught sight of the officers inside the building, he bailed quicker than shit." He put his hand over his mouth for a second. "Sorry. I have a potty mouth sometimes."

"That's okay. I've heard worse. After my mom's had a bottle of wine, she does that too." The adults smiled and Cole smiled back, but he was anxious to hear the conclusion of the story. "So, were you right? Did he try to run out of the back?"

"He sure did. And I was there waiting for the scumbag. When he opened that door and saw me standing there, I think he about crapped his pants. He almost ran right into me. I had my gun drawn but he got right up in my face very quickly. Before I even knew what was going on, he had slapped the gun from my hand. And he was kind of a big guy too, which I didn't expect."

Unknown to Jeb and Cole, Gretchen had been standing at the doorway, desperately wanting to see her baby and make sure he was doing okay. When Dr. Weinstein noticed her presence, she put a finger up, which Gretchen acknowledged by backing off.

"Oh no. If you didn't have your gun, what could you do? Oh wait. You had another officer with you, right?"

"I did, but he was standing watch at the corner of the building and didn't even see the guy come out, so he was no help in that moment. Lucky for me, I'm pretty strong. I work out at the gym almost every day." Jeb flexed his right arm, revealing his bulging bicep. "So, I did the only thing I could think to do in that situation. I charged right at him. I put my head down and slammed right into him, sending us both flying into the brick wall behind him. He didn't even see it coming. When he hit the wall, his head whipped back so hard, I could hear his skull crack and he was out like a light."

"Wow. You're super tough." Cole had taken

the bait and was feeling as confident as he ever would that things would work out fine and that he would be safe if he revealed everything he knew about his abduction, the monster in the cabin, and the other children. Without warning, his attention quickly turned to the memories of his time away and his mood shifted.

"I like to believe that in the end, the good guys will win because we have right on our side." Jeb saw the fear in Cole's eyes and decided to take one last shot of getting something, anything from him. "Like with that bad man, when a victim helped us out, we need you to help us now. You have nothing to be scared of. We'll protect you, keep you safe, and if someone ever took you again and did bad things, we'll take them down."

A memory of the bad man from the cabin popped into Cole's head. On his second day in captivity, Cole chose to argue with something his captor said, who retaliated with a firm backhand slap across Cole's face, sending him flailing to the hardwood floor. That was the first and last time he challenged his master, the day an unwavering fear in another human being took hold. Before that day, Cole had never experienced a physical assault, let alone such a violent one.

Out of nowhere, Cole burst into tears. He heard the words Detective Jebsen said, but as an eleven-year-old child, he could only extrapolate so much. The overwhelming sensations he experienced were fear and doubt and he could not conquer them, not that day, no matter how much he believed Jeb.

Detective Jebsen let out a sigh, and he and Dr. Weinstein exchanged shrugs and confused looks as the doctor stepped to the end of the bed.

Before she could get a word out, Gretchen barged into the room and made her way to Cole's side, opposite where the detective was seated. She held Cole's hand, ran her fingers through his hair, and rubbed his head to comfort him.

"Everything is going to be fine baby." Gretchen turned her attention to the adults. "This interview is over." She overheard most of the session and fully understood what they were trying to accomplish, but if there was one thing she could not tolerate, it was hearing and seeing her son in such emotional turmoil.

"We understand how you must feel. Obviously, Cole has been through one heck of an ordeal," Dr. Weinstein said.

"No! I don't think you do know how it feels. My son was gone, away from his family, his life, his school, for seventeen days. Seventeen days. He says he can't remember much. That's just going to have to be enough. How much torture can you put my son through before it's enough?"

"Ma'am. Please. I," Detective Jebsen said

before being interrupted by Gretchen.

"I'll tell you how much is enough. It was enough about five minutes ago. He needs time to relax and sort things out. Try to put yourself in his shoes for one minute. One damn minute." She turned and kissed Cole on his forehead. He had finally stopped crying but was still sobbing softly, using the corner of his sheet to wipe the tears from his face.

"This interrogation is over. I'd like to talk to you both in the hallway please," Gretchen said, wide-eyed and leaving no room for discussion in her tone.

They knew there was no point arguing with a lioness protecting her cub with that kind of voracity. Without another word, they left the room to talk in the hallway.

"I sympathize with your work in this investigation, Detective Jebsen, but none of us know what Cole has been through, and it hasn't even been twenty-four hours since I got him back. I feel like he needs time to get his bearings before any more questioning can take place." Jeb tried to speak but Gretchen put her hand up and continued with barely a breath. "Now, before you say anything, know that I do understand how critical the timing is, and that there are two other children missing and every minute counts. Believe me, I get it. But I'm asking you, as a mother who knows her son, to give us a day and you can ask him anything you want." Gretchen put up a firm index finger. "One day ... and you can come to the house and see if he remembers anything more. Deal?"

"Sounds like you're not giving me much choice," Jeb said. "I just hope, for the sake of the other two missing children, should their disappearance end up be related, that this doesn't turn out to be a big mistake. You don't want that on your conscience ... and neither do I."

"I do feel terrible about those other two children. I do. As a mother who thought she lost her son, I actually can imagine what their parents are dealing with, but we don't know if they are connected to Cole's disappearance, and I simply can't worry too much about that, not in this moment. I need to do what I think is best for Cole, and for the next twenty-four hours, I believe isolation and some time at home away from all this mess would be the best thing for him. I'm sorry but that's my final decision. Now, if you don't mind, I'd like to be with my son."

Detective Jebsen reluctantly nodded and pulled a business card from his inside coat pocket. He handed it to Gretchen. "Please call me tomorrow and we'll set up a time."

"I will. And I appreciate your efforts in investigating what happened to Cole. I want nothing more than to discover the truth and for you to find the bastard that did this." Gretchen turned abruptly and entered the room.

"They've been through a lot but they'll come around," Dr. Weinstein said. "He's definitely withholding something. Perhaps the memories are slow to return, but they will. We both understand how easy it is to compartmentalize such a traumatic life event. It's a coping and survival mechanism."

"I know. I was just so close to breaking through with him. Damn."

From over Dr. Weinstein's shoulder, Detective Jebsen spotted a uniformed officer come around the corner in a hurry.

"Detective. We have crews on the scene of a now smoldering fire east of town. You might want to come and check it out."

"And why is that officer?"

Befuddled by the question, the officer answered, "Well, they think they've found some animal and some ... human remains, sir. It's just a couple miles from where the Redman boy was discovered."

"They *think* they've found ... or *have* found, son?"

"Definitely ... have ... found," said the officer in staccato, his head bobbing with each word. "There is just a question of how many."

"Oh Christ. I'm done here anyway," Jeb said. He turned his attention back to the doctor. "Thanks, Emma. I'll call you tomorrow after I arrange something with Ms. Redman." Jeb immediately followed the officer out.

"You bet. I'll talk to you then."

7

Friday, November 9th, 2012 – 3:43 p.m.
Unknown Location

Cole opened his eyes to darkness and a searing pain, pounding like a bass drum across his entire head. As he moved his left hand to the back of his head to rub a sore spot, he noticed something odd brushing his elbow. He lifted his arm up from whatever it was touching, nervous about the predicament he might be in and the strange, cold metal beneath his arm. He took a moment to try and gather his thoughts. The last thing he remembered was standing at his front door, then nothing.

Using only the fingers on his left hand, Cole cautiously touched the area next to his body. Whatever it was, there were a lot of them. He brushed some aside until he felt a spongy canvas material with metal tubing on the edge of it. A cot? It reminded him of the ones his office building kept in a little corner room that doubled as a makeshift nurse's station, always ready for anyone who might need to lie down if they happened to get sick at work. Am I at work? The room was too dark for Cole to know for sure.

Chills suddenly raced down his spine and extended to his limbs as the damp, frigid air of the room finally caught up to his still awakening body. He shivered and picked up one of the unusual metal objects scattered all over the cot. He ran the object between his thumb, index, and middle fingers. It was small, maybe two inches long, one end slender, the other wider. The ridges on the slender end revealed it all. The object was a key. He dropped the key and picked up another and another and another. Every object on the bed was a key. Some were typical deadbolt keys, others more like car keys with the thicker plastic ends. Others seemed like they were made of plastic and more like a toy, while some were old-fashioned skeleton types.

Cole had the sensation of his heart dropping in

his chest, his stomach nauseous. The breath in his lungs disappeared, forcing him to take short and quick inhales to get oxygen. Instinctively, he put a hand to his chest to feel the beat of his heart.

Without warning, a bright light emerged from the center of the ceiling of the room. Cole closed his eyes. Just as quickly as the light arrived, it came back down but stayed on in a low, yellowish-orange dim. When Cole peeled his eyes open, he could see the room for the first time.

The four concrete walls were each ten-feet across and ten-feet tall. The cot on which Cole awoke was against the wall in one corner, a heating and cooling vent above the head of the cot, near the ceiling. Coinciding with the light coming to life, warm air flowed from the vent.

In the opposite corner, diagonally from the cot sat a small aluminum chair with Cole's jacket draped across the back, a chair much like one might see in a prison cafeteria. In the corner to Cole's left, a dingy, white five-gallon bucket sat on the floor. The wall to the right of the metal chair had a large steel door directly in the middle of it, completely rusted over with a curved steel pull handle and a keyhole plate beneath that. A simple, plastic white kitchen clock hung above the door.

As terrifying as the room appeared to Cole, the

most disturbing aspect had already revealed itself. The entire floor of the room and the cot he laid on was covered with keys, thousands of different keys, in all shapes and sizes. There were brass and silver ordinary house keys, rainbow colored toy keys like the ones given to babies and toddlers, rusty skeleton keys, various automobile keys, smaller padlock keys, and train station locker keys - all in every size, shape, and color.

Confusion racked Cole's brain. He suddenly had the urge to vomit, so he shuffled off the bed, sending keys scattering about with each movement. As he took scrambled and unbalanced steps across the key-covered floor toward the bucket, his feet continually slid from under him. He lost his balance and came down on his left hip, but his face safely made it to the bucket as he spit up stomach acid. With nothing else to release, he dry-heaved half a dozen times before pulling away. His eyes watered from the exertion, and perhaps, from the fear.

He had no idea how he ended up in the strange room of keys, but he had a pretty good idea how he might get out, though the task looked daunting. He did have one big question. *Who the hell did this to me and why?*

Cole sat on the floor trying to calm down. He rubbed his forehead and started to weep.

"I knew there was something weird about that

fuckin' van," he whispered with self-admonishment. "I really need to trust my instincts."

Still sitting, he shifted ninety degrees and looked around the room to fully absorb his surroundings. The first thing that caught his eye was the chair straight ahead of him. The seat was the only flat surface in the room that was not entirely covered in keys, but more importantly, it held his jacket. *Cell phone.*

"Shit. That's right. Before I ended up here, I was standing at my front door because I had left my damn cell phone at home. Ahhh. Idiot." He kept his voice quiet. "Not that whoever did this would have left me my phone, but still." So, why leave the jacket at all? He then remembered the bizarre interoffice mail he received the day before - a manila envelope he shoved into the inside pocket of that jacket, an envelope he had yet to open.

On his hands and knees, he gingerly crawled to the chair, trying not to slip on the keys as he moved. When he arrived at the chair, he checked each pocket for his phone, just to be safe. He wondered how stupid he would feel if the cell phone had been there all along and he not even bothered to look. Luck was not on his side. He pulled out the only item in the jacket. As he suspected, the small manila envelope he received at work was still there. The words were written with a red marker, the envelope flap held closed with the metal clasp folded flat.

Cole pinched the metal clasps up, pulled open the flap, and looked inside the envelope. White paper was the only thing he could see, so he removed it, discovering it was a single piece of printer or copy paper, folded in half. There were words printed on the upper half of the outside section of the paper: In a room full of Keys, oNly One Will set you free. Watch the clock ... tick tock tick.

The capital letters embedded in the message revealed the words: I KNOW.

In a room full of Keys, oNly One Will set you free.

Watch the clock ... tick tock tick.

Cole pondered the meaning of the letter and the not so subtle message within the words. Clearly, whoever perpetrated his kidnapping and created the elaborate room of keys knew about his past, like many did, as his disappearance and reappearance on the side of the road seventeen days later was in all the papers and on all the local news channels. There was, however, more to the story than anyone truly knew, details that only four people had any knowledge of, two of which were buried and long gone. A room full of keys on the twentieth anniversary of his escape meant one thing - the pool of suspects had narrowed considerably. There were secrets that had never been revealed, choices made by Cole that ate away at his soul every day for twenty years, and in the moment, he wasn't so sure he didn't deserve whatever horrible fate lay ahead of him in that room.

He placed the envelope and the letter on the seat of the chair and just sat there thinking about how much he even cared to fight for his freedom. *Maybe karma is finally catching up to me. I imagine whoever is doing this wants to see me struggle, to squirm, to panic. But what if I don't indulge? What if I just sit here and do ... nothing? What if I just accept my fate and not play the game?*

Cole got on his feet using the chair to brace himself. He spotted what appeared to be a small window, eighteen inches across by ten inches tall, in the middle of the wall between the bucket and the chair. He stepped to it and peered in but found only blackness. He wondered if someone was watching from the other side.

"Hello in there. I don't know who you are but I don't want to play this game. If you want to kill me, just go ahead and do it. I don't really care anymore." Cole stopped and knocked on the window three times with his left fist. "Hey! Show yourself and let's just get this over with!"

He took a step back and waited for a response but none came.

"Well ... I'm just gonna sit here and wait." Cole stepped lightly on the keys as he made his way back to the cot where he brushed all the keys off, planted his butt, and sat staring at the door, waiting for something, anything.

Thirty minutes passed without movement or sound from Cole, or from outside the room. Cole did not waste the time. In case he changed his mind, he studied the room. There were so many keys on the floor, at first, he had no clue where to start. As he thought about it, one quick way to narrow it down crossed his mind. Even though there were thousands of keys, there were only roughly eight or nine different kinds. He figured he could sort all of them into separate piles by type and that would at least be a good place to start.

He turned his attention to the door. After looking at it for a few minutes, another obvious fact dawned on him. The keyhole beneath the steel handle made it pretty clear which keys it could not be, further shrinking what seemed like endless possibilities. The challenge of the situation was quickly diminishing, and some confidence started to build toward his eventual getaway. He doubted it would be as simple as that, although, he hoped it would be.

On the verge of putting into action the first part of his plan to get the door open, Cole noticed a strange smell. He followed the intensity with his nose, leading him to the vent above the cot. A smoky mist poured from behind the grate. He put his hand to his mouth and nose but it was too late. He choked and gasped for air before he started to cough uncontrollably. For thirty seconds he fought the gas, but once it fully penetrated his lungs, he fell hard to the cot, out cold.

.8

Wednesday, October 31st, 2012 – 11:08 p.m.
Unknown Location

A figure sat in the shadows of a room on a rough, wood desk chair built in the 1960s, a hoodie obscuring their face. A single, small light shined directly at the work in front of them. The eight-foot banquet table shoved against the wall served as their laboratory. To the left, an older model Windows XP desktop computer stood tall, a keyboard and a mouse on a pad pushed in front of it. An almond colored CRT monitor sat perfectly centered. The right side of the table held a secondhand inkjet printer of the same era, used only with black ink. In front of the printer was a nearly full pack of twenty pound copy paper with one end torn open, and a package of six-inch by nine-inch manila envelopes with one removed.

The faceless person enjoyed the squeak of the red marker as it scraped across the manila envelope, leaving behind a first and last name, and the number 'five' with three periods following it.

Their heart had grown callous over the years, a result of painful past events that festered and soured, their path in life forced to change, leaving no room for better choices, no chance for a better life.

The person recapped the marker and placed it aside, staring at their right hand, the last two digits missing from a time during the past they only wish they could forget. A raging fire continued to build in their belly, lava oozing from every pour, white hot flames burning behind their eyes. The pain of those memories could never be forgotten with such an obvious and disgusting daily reminder. This person had learned to write again without the fingers, and it presented no further handicap, however, the sight of the scarred-over nubs and the claw-like remaining fingers put a constant pit in their stomach, an undying link to an excruciating past.

With the envelope prepared exactly as planned, they reached over to the printer tray and removed a single piece of paper printed five minutes earlier. They read the words printed across the lower half of the page, then re-read them a dozen more times, carefully sounding out each word in their head. The message had to be perfect.

They folded the paper in half horizontally and slid it inside the already prepared manila envelope, folding down the flap and using the metal clasp to secure it.

"One down, four to go," the person whispered.

The keyboard and mouse slid easily across the laminated surface of the table, the movement of the mouse bringing the monitor back to life with a slow fade-in from black to blue then to the white of a blank document, ready to be typed.

A spiral notebook just to the person's right contained all the words they had conceived over the prior months of the planning phase, words that would be typed into the computer and printed for effect. With each document created and saved, the printer mechanisms squeaked and chirped with tiny plastic gears and rubber cylinders turning.

The third note became stuck in the rollers as it inched out of the printer. It wasn't the first time the out-of-date machine malfunctioned. With a finite amount of financial resources, they counted on refurbishing older equipment picked up on the curb or from thrift stores, keeping them running longer than most people could have, or would ever care to. And even though this person did not grow up with computers readily available, their self-taught skills had surpassed the average first-level I.T. support person.

"Stupid piece of crap!" They struck the side of the printer then grabbed the end of the stuck piece of paper, tugging at it until it came free. The second attempt at printing the note was trouble free, and the rest went through without any problem.

After midnight, the computer was shutdown, the desk lamp turned off, and the chair tucked under the table's edge. Other chores had to be done in another room of the building, other duties that needed attention. The day was growing close for the first steps of their master plan to unfold. The time for a reckoning was near.

About a week later –

The train station hummed with commuter chaos. People darted here and there, some stood in long lines waiting for their trains, others huddling around the baggage areas. The clack and screech of trains starting and stopping muffled the other noises, the conversations, the announcements.

The brisk morning air forced the person dressed all in black to wear more layers than was normally comfortable for the job at hand. Over the years, they had become an expert at the art of picking pockets. A mentor of theirs taught all the lessoned needed to be good and not get caught. *Busy areas work best, don't dally, keep your face obscured.*

In a good week, four to five hundred dollars could be had, mostly in small bills, just from picking wallets at a couple of train stations and shopping malls. This small-risk, high-reward effort made for a great income supplement.

On that day, the wallets were not the target. Back at the warehouse, there were a couple of black, thirty-two gallon trashcans that needed to be filled, and the time for putting the plan in action was drawing near. The preparations had been ongoing for nearly three years, and by best guess, one last morning of gathering keys to top of the trashcans would do.

Of course, lifting keys instead of wallets was especially tricky, as the jingle was sure to reveal all. Gripping them tightly together was the best technique for quelling the noise.

With head covered, the person stood near a

post pretending to read a newspaper they picked up as they entered the station. The method was simple. When someone walked by that looked like an easy target, someone with an open purse or a jacket with large pockets, the pickpocket would start to fold the newspaper and step into the unknowing victim. The bump occurred simultaneously with a slip of a hand. The person's missing fingers on their right hand made it much less likely to be detected, though snatching with just three fingers took some serious practice.

The work was quick. Not even three seconds passed before the operation was complete. A quick apology followed by a move to another location rebooted the entire process. On the final day of prep and a successful grab of eight sets of keys, it was time to leave.

Another method for acquiring keys was to simply purchase them from hardware stores, uncut, right off the rack. Money was tight but at fifty cents to a dollar per key, it became necessary to supplement some this way. Every few weeks, the person shoved fifty or so of the blanks into a shopping basket at a hardware store, a different store every time so as not to arouse suspicions. Over time, several thousand keys were gathered in this manner.

To get the really old and unusual keys, they counted on a clerk at a local pawn shop located around the corner, just a few blocks down from the building the person called home.

This clerk had a certain affinity for photographs showing naked children being tortured and sexually assaulted, a specialty of the seeker of keys. An arrangement was made whereby photos would be provided in exchange for any old keys sold to the pawn store. The twisted and vile clerk leapt at the chance, and upon seeing the first three images, would be a reliable and trusted source for several years of many large sets of keys.

***

Back at the warehouse, both home and lab, the hooded figure hovered over the two black trashcans, methodically pulling each key from the rings they were attached to and dropping them one by one with the rest. Both cans were filled roughly four inches from the top rim. Most of them the uncut hardware store variety.

When the final key was placed in the right-hand barrel, the person nodded with pleasure at the accomplishment. They took one, long, deep breath then exhaled quickly.

"It's time to finish prepping the room. Tomorrow is the big day."

9

Saturday, November 10th, 2012 – 4:10 a.m.
Unknown Location

A soft buzz of electricity hummed from the dim ceiling light as Cole opened his eyes. His throat burned with each swallow. Whatever noxious gas choked him into unconsciousness hours earlier had burned his throat. In the stillness of the room, the clock above the door clicked loud and annoying.

Cole sat up, desperately needing some water to help soothe his throat. When he looked across the room, he spotted something new. In the precise middle of the floor, a small area of keys had been cleared away, and in their place, another manila envelope, and next to that, a large gas station style plastic beverage cup with a lid and a straw, and a small disposal bowl with a plastic spoon resting across the top.

The clock read 4:12, but he had no idea if it was morning or afternoon, only that it was near four o'clock when he first woke up in the room, so he made the assumption it had been at least twelve hours since his kidnapping. He was certain more than twenty minutes had passed. However long it had been, he knew one thing - he was starving. Cole hoped the contents of the bowl would at least be edible. The presence of food did make him feel a little better. He figured the perpetrator of his capture wouldn't likely feed him if the intent was to kill him because, what would be the point. That was something, even if just a small kernel of hope.

Cole got on his feet and stretched his arms and back. "That cot is the most uncomfortable fucking thing I've ever slept on in my life. My back is starting to spaz out." He set his gaze on the little window on the opposite wall, as if he were looking into the eyes of the kidnapper. "You could have at least put a mattress in here. Asshole." Cole made a final twist of his back before walking to the center of the room.

To be on the safe side, he decided to read the

envelope first, just in case there was pertinent information inside about the food, like it was poisoned or rotten. He bent over, picked it up, and read the face, but not out loud.

Every assist comes with a price. This one costs you: (HEAT, FOOD, WATER, LIFE) 4 ...

The word heat had a red X over it.

No sooner had he read the words when he noticed the light stream of warm air that was coming from the vent above the bed ceased. Assuming he was still in Michigan, he immediately knew what it would mean to have no heat in a room made of concrete, in November, in the upper Midwest.

He opened the envelope with nervous fingers, terrified to find out what was inside, but he was so hungry, he needed to know if the bowl contained something safe to eat. Once again, the envelope contained a single piece of white copy paper, folded in half so it fit perfectly in the envelope. It read: when chaos reigns, will You save yOurself or save them? sort oUt the mess, onLy then will you sEe truth. one For you and one for Them. Watch the clock ... tick tock.

when chaos reigns, will You save yOurself or save

them? sort oUt the mess, onLy then will you sEe truth.

one For you and one for Them.

Watch the clock ... tick tock.

He didn't even read the entire note. The larger letters scattered throughout, 'YOU LEFT', ran through his head two dozen times before he could bring himself to move forward.

"Who are you? Why are doing this to me?" Cole shouted, tipping his head back in frustration and grinding his teeth. At the top of his lungs he yelled, "What do you want from me?" The sound did not travel, instead it filled the room for a second with his sharp tone. His chest heaved as he stood in silence, waiting for a response, not that he actually expected one.

In that quiet moment, his stomach rumbled so loud, someone could have heard it from thirty feet away. He could no longer wait, so, he walked over to the cot, placed the note and the envelope down there, and returned to the cup, bowl and spoon. He brought them back to the cot and sat down to eat and drink. He took a three-second long sip from the straw, happy to discover it was just water, so far as he could tell. He placed the cup on the floor and brought the bowl to his face to smell its contents. There was no distinguishable odor, which worried him.

"Great." Cole shook his head but decided he just didn't have any choice. He had to eat. A headache was already creeping in from the lack of caffeine, so getting any sustenance was going to be critical in keeping his brain functioning. He knew if he was going to have any chance of getting out of there alive, he would need to be thinking clearly, and starvation was a sure way to lose cognition.

He grazed the top of the porridge with the spoon to get a little taster, bringing it to the tip of his tongue. "Oh god. Oatmeal with no milk and sugar. And ice cold. How positively disgusting. Thanks a lot." He ate the small amount of oatmeal off the spoon, scraping the utensil with his teeth and swallowing without chewing, careful not to let it touch his tongue.

He pushed through the rest of the bowl in the same fashion, finishing the entire thing in less than two minutes. Afterwards, he sipped down half the water from his cup before placing it under the cot to save for later, just in case he received nothing else for a while.

With his hunger satisfied, at least temporarily, the chill of the room again attacked his skin. I'm *not sure what's worse, no heat or no food? I gotta get up and move around.*

Cole picked up the letter and reread it, but more carefully this time. "Sort out the mess? Well, that seems pretty obvious." Cole got up, leaving the note on the cot.

He walked over to the door to investigate the lock when something dawned on him. "I can't believe I didn't even try the handle." With a tiny grain of optimism, he put his fingers around the handle and gave it tug. There was no movement. The door was locked. He grabbed the handle with both hands and gripped it tightly before giving it one, big pull with every ounce of strength and energy he could muster. The door did not budge, not one bit.

"Damn it! Let me out of here you fucking bastard!" With his left fist, he pounded on the metal door six times while screaming, "Help! Is anybody out there? Help!"

Cole turned around, leaned against the door, and slumped to the floor, utterly exhausted. He placed his hand on his heaving chest as he tried to catch his breath. He caressed the key hanging around his neck too.

"No. There's no way." He locked his eyes on the key and chain around his neck. He quickly pulled it around his head, turned to the door, and from his knees, inserted the key into the hole. It fit but was tight. He rocked it left and right. The lock did not budge.

"Shit! Well, it was worth a try, however unlikely." He removed the key and placed the necklace back over his head then turned around and planted his butt back down.

"Okay. Think Cole, think. There are a ton of keys all over this place but only one is going to fit this lock." He pulled away from the door, turned to face it, studying the lock. One thing stood out immediately. The lock was old. Of all the different types of keys in the room, only the skeleton keys would have a chance of opening the door, so he figured that would be a good place to start.

In an effort to stay warm with movement, Cole stood up and started to do exactly what the note suggested he do - sort out the mess. He thought the corner of the room by the bucket would be the best place to throw all the keys the he knew would not work. All the skeleton keys would be piled up near the chair.

With a sense of urgency, Cole used his foot to clear a space around the chair to put all the skeleton keys that did not fit after he tried them, then he did the same in the opposite corner, first moving his bathroom bucket to the floor at the end of the cot, not far from the door.

Starting next to the cot, he began picking up handfuls of keys, tossing the bad ones in the corner and leaving the viable candidates on the cot with the intention of eliminating them one by one.

After an hour, he had what he estimated to be four hundred skeleton keys on the cot and a rather large heap of discarded ones in the corner.

"I can't believe in all this time I've only cleared this much floor area." He stared down at the roughly three-foot wide stretch of floor next to the six-foot long cot. *Progress*, he thought, *but not nearly enough.*

"Guess I'll just try all these and see if I get lucky. Gotta start somewhere."

He placed ten keys in his right hand and walked over to the door. One by one, handful after handful, he inserted each key into the lock, carefully attempting to turn the key in both directions, finally placing all of them from the first round into a small mound by the chair.

Cole sighed deeply after failing to find the right key. With two hours having passed since he ate the oatmeal, his vigorous expenditure of energy and the cold air zapped him further, so he decided to rest on the cot for a bit. He snatched his jacket off the chair and laid out on the cot, bunching up the jacket to use as a pillow. This was his best effort to make the cot more comfortable. His neck felt the difference, but his back still ached.

Within minutes, he could no longer fight the icy chill of the air, so he removed the jacket from behind his head and used it as a makeshift blanket, covering his torso right up to his chin.

Thoughts about escape, his own bed, and a good, hot cup of coffee raced through his mind as his eye lids grew too heavy to fight.

10

Sunday, November 8th, 1992 – 1:38 p.m.
Rural Ingham County, Michigan

The squad car turned left off of County Road
1100 onto a lightly graveled and dirt path, single
car wide, which cut through a crowded area of
trees, a road most people would never notice if it
weren't for the small wooden sign near the main
road that read: No Trespassing. Close behind was
Detective Jebsen in his dark brown 1991 Chevy
Caprice unmarked car.

Jeb pondered everything Cole had revealed
during their questioning, which the detective
acknowledged wasn't much. *Two miles from where
the boy was found, we have a remote cabin razed to the
ground. There are human remains present. There are still*

two other children missing, and they all go to the same school. He wondered what the odds would actually be that they were not connected. In his experience, coincidence did occur on cases from time to time, but nine out of ten times, those coincidences were really connections. With the information from Cole starting out to be a dead end, any new prospects for answers in his disappearance and that of the other two missing children were welcome, even with the potentially grim nature of this new discovery.

After a three-minute drive at fifteen miles per hour, the vehicles arrived at a partial clearing where three squad cars, a fire engine, an ambulance, and the fire chief's SUV were already present, spinning lights bouncing from surface to surface. A man in black and gold gear combed through the rubble with a shovel, no doubt looking for more remains. The flames had been extinguished and only a few tiny smoke stacks billowed lightly from various spots within. Another firefighter worked on breaking up those hotspots and putting them out.

When Jeb parked and emerged from his car, the smoky char reminded him of an old campfire that had been doused by rain. A gathering of officials had convened near the fire chief's vehicle, so he made his way to the group to get an update on any findings.

"Jeb," said fire chief Hank Jefferson, waving as Jeb walked toward them, interrupting whatever conversation had been in progress. "I'll be back in sec," the chief informed his group.

Hank stepped away from the semi-circle and met Jeb halfway. They exchanged a firm handshake, like two longtime associates, but they were also good friends outside of the work environment.

"Hank. I see you got this one under control."

"Oh yeah. Not a biggie but definitely gasoline accelerated."

Jeb nodded. "Bodies?"

"Just one so far ... human anyway. Small, likely a child."

"Damn. Non-human too?"

"Yeah. There are a few small animal ones. Hopefully, we'll find out more when Beth gets here. Otherwise, the lab will have to sort it out. I hear you questioned the boy found on the side of the road not far from here. How'd that go?"

"Not as good as I would've liked. Kid is scared shitless, which is to be expected," Jeb said, shrugging his shoulders.

"Sure."

"He claims he can't really remember anything, that he was ... out of it ... most of the seventeen days, but clearly he's holding back. I'm supposed to go over and talk to him again at his home

Richard A. Powell II

tomorrow. His mother, of course, is being difficult. Hopefully, I'll squeeze a little more out of him, but this fire is worrisome. We may be too late."

"Hard not to think these two are connected, especially with two other kids still missing."

"I was just thinking the same thing. You find any other evidence?" Jeb turned his eyes to the blackened leftovers of the building. Images of children held captive by a menacing psychotic streamed through his mind. He shook the imagery from his head and looked back to his friend.

"Not really. Place was a cabin of some kind, probably used for hunting. There are remnants of a few beds, a sink, not much else. Everything burned up pretty good. And with the gas, our initial assessment is arson. Beth is on the way but I doubt she'll be able to determine anything out here, not without a closer look back at the lab."

"Well, we need to figure out who owns this property. That'd be a good start."

"I believe Joe is working on that. Soon as he got here, he contacted someone at the station to start looking into it." Just as Hank finished his sentence, Joe Pagano joined them. "Speaking of," Hank added.

"Detective. Nasty mess we got here," Joe said with raised eyebrows.

"No doubt. Redman boy wasn't much help either. Like I was just telling Hank, I'm going to question him again tomorrow. His mother freaked out, making us wait a day before we see him again."

"I imagine he's quite traumatized. He give you *anything*?"

"A dark room. A man. Ran for a long time before passing out on the side of the road. Says he was in a haze the whole time and that he didn't even know seventeen days had passed. Claims he didn't see anyone else and that he doesn't know the Simpson kids. He's scared and definitely holding back a bit. Like I said, I'll try again tomorrow."

"I got people searching property records so we can figure out who owns this place."

"That's what Hank just said. Good. Let me know the second you figure anything out." Jeb looked again to the remains of the cabin. "I'm gonna snoop around the grounds a little until the coroner gets here." He turned back to Hank and offered his hand. They shook. "Thanks, Hank. I'll be in touch."

"You bet. Good luck. Looks like you got a tough one on your hands."

"We'll get it sorted out."

Hank walked back to the group near his vehicle where he immediately engaged in the conversation already in progress.

"You need anything from me right now?" Joe asked.

"You have anyone talking to neighbors of this property?"

"Ummm ... there are a couple of farmhouses, one east, one west, both a decent distance away, so no. Should we?"

"Hell yes!"

Joe was a detective too, but a young one and he was still learning all the finer of points of investigation. He counted on Jeb to guide him and wasn't afraid to ask questions but that didn't stop Jeb from reacting in a way that often made Joe feel like he should have known better.

"These rural property owners tend to know one another, even with all this acreage between them. So, please get on that, personally. See what you can dig up on that front. Get back to me right away if anything pops."

"Yes sir. I'll take care of it."

"All right then. I'll see you back at the station."

Joe hustled away to his car and within two minutes was gone to complete his task.

Jeb walked around the perimeter of the cabin, staying a few feet away as he tried to avoid stepping in the muddy, ashy puddles. His gaze stayed low, mostly just in front of his feet in search of a cigarette butt, a partially scorched shoe tread, a glass bottle, or better yet, as he hoped, a stone tablet with someone's name, address, and phone number etched onto it. *That would sure make it easier*, he thought.

He had already made up his mind that something wicked was going on at the location - he only wished they had found the place sooner. Every minute counted but he didn't blame Cole. He realized that even if the Redman boy had provided more useful information, they would have been too late to do anything about the burned-up cabin and the child who may have died there. Someone was up to no good. That seemed a certainty. A successful burn and run and an uncooperative child were giant obstacles. Getting on the right track was becoming an increasingly daunting task, and always one step behind would be a hard fact to overcome in such a time-sensitive case.

Jeb made his way once around the tarred and soggy debris just in time to meet the coroner as she exited her car. He failed to discover anything useful. Perhaps she could have some insight once she examined the bones.

"Jeb," Bethany Klotz greeted. She was the elected county coroner serving her fourth term. She stood about the same height as Jeb, two inches under six feet and was a marathon runner, thin, tanning bed bronze too, with long black hair tied into a ponytail to keep it out of the way while she worked. She carried a black leather bag, firm on the sides like an old medical bag, except hers was shiny and new - a birthday gift from her husband.

"Beth. Glad you're here. We got nothing so far. I'm hoping you can pull a rabbit out of your ass."

Beth gave him smirk. "You mean out of my hat?"

"I don't know. This has been a shit day, so ass seems more fitting." He shook his head. "Sorry. Freudian slip I suppose."

"No need to be sorry. Missing kids, burned down cabin, charred skeletons. That *is* shit." She cut right to the job at hand. "Point me in the right direction."

Jeb caught sight of her galoshes. "I see you brought the right footwear. I came straight from the hospital, so," he shrugged.

"Too many years on this job not to remember the boots. Damn sloppy walking around once the fire boys have had their fun."

They approached what was left of the cabin and Jeb pointed to an area on the left side, not far from what would have been the back wall.

"Those are the human ones." He pointed again but to the other side. "There are other animal ones too, squirrels we think, on the far right."

Jeb watched Beth step slow and deliberate, settling each foot down solidly before taking another step forward. The firefighters had trampled a path to the bones, so it was relatively clear, but what she really wanted to avoid was slipping and falling. She once said if she had a dollar for every time someone slipped and fell at a crime scene, whether it be on blood, entrails, or water, she could buy a new Gucci purse every year. She promised herself after her first term as coroner that she would never let it happen to her, and to date, the promise was unbroken.

Beth easily found the skeleton. It stuck out like a wolf in the middle of a flock of sheep. She placed her bag on the ground after spotting the only clear area not littered with burnt debris. She squatted down, working hard to keep her balance. A quick survey of the remains revealed nothing obvious as to cause of death, at least other than fire. A closer investigation in the lab would be needed to fully understand how the person died, if that could ever be uncovered.

The only thing she was sure of was that the size of the skeleton revealed an age range of six to ten years old, depending on the sex, which she could not determine by sight on a pre-pubescent skeleton, as the bone differences between men and women do not become evident until the teenage years. In men, the bones are thicker and the pelvic area is too narrow to pass a baby, whereas, the ribcage of women tends to be narrower, the bones are generally thinner, and the pelvic region is wider, for obvious reasons.

After checking out the animal remains, she returned to Jeb who was waiting patiently just outside the burn field.

"It's a shame. Someone so young," Beth said.

"Anything useful?" Jeb asked.

"Not really. Probably eight, maybe nine years old. No way to know if they died in the fire or beforehand, at least not until I can inspect the bones at the lab. Sex undetermined. And you were right, the other bones are squirrels."

"Definitely fits the profile for one of the other kids. That can't be a coincidence. My guess, when the Redman kid escaped, the perp panicked, killed one or both of the other kids, and burned down the cabin to cover his tracks."

"That sounds reasonable but we know how unreasonable a perp like this can be. What about the other missing child? Taken?"

"That's one big problem. We're still missing one kid and unless we figure out who this person is, we have no idea where to look next. This damn fire isn't going to give us anything, I'm sure. Hopefully, the property records will yield something. Cross our fingers." He did just that.

"I hope so too. I'll let you know the second I

figure anything out about the bones. I'll send the boys in to extract them and we'll get them back to the lab. I'll start the exam immediately. I know time is of the essence on this one."

"Thanks Beth. I really appreciate that."

"You bet," Beth finished with a wave and off she went to have the paramedics load the bones and transport them. She stopped after a few steps and turned back to Jeb. "Somebody did mention the chains to you, right?"

"Chains?"

"Yes. Not sure if anyone else noticed it. The skeleton had a metal cuff with a small padlock around one wrist. It was attached to a heavy-duty chain that was secured to a ring bolted to the concrete floor. With all the char, it wasn't that obvious, unless you're really looking."

"No shit! Oh boy. This just got ten times more interesting." Jeb rubbed his temples.

"And," she gave him a look that piqued his curiosity even more. "There are two other cuffs and chains not attached to anything. A pretty clear picture is starting to form here I'd say."

"Yep. Three kids, three chains. Damn it! Where's the third kid?"

Beth shook her head. She waved again and walked away, leaving Jeb without another word. It was clear he was already deep in thought anyway.

Detective Jebsen pondered the scene, his theories, and Cole. *Where's the other body? Did you keep one? If so, why? Why not take both? Why not kill both? Maybe you already killed the other one. But where's the body?* He repeated the last question two more times.

He didn't have the answer to any of the questions and it pissed him off. He didn't want these missing child cases to turn out like most of the others, with disturbing and unpleasant endings. When Cole was discovered, Jeb held the tiniest speck of hope for a different resolution than usual. For once, maybe the children would be found, mostly unharmed, and they would be reunited with their families, their friends, their once peaceful childhoods. They would be able to grow up, go to college, get married, and have children of their own. That image was fading from the hopeful part of Jeb's mind.

One kid, he thought, *did get lucky, but two of them did not. One of them, it appeared, had died in a dark place, an evil place, where no child should ever have to go, let alone spend their last days.* Another one's fate remained undetermined.

The person responsible needed to be stopped. Jeb wanted nothing more as he thought about what kind of person could have done such a despicable thing. *How evil does a person have to be to do something like this? These are kids for God's sake.*

How does someone even get to a point in their life where they can be so heartless?

11

Tuesday, June 15th, 1965 – 9:54 a.m.
Rockford, Illinois

The neighborhood looked rough, with crumbling buildings and sidewalks to match, rusty abandoned cars, most at least a decade old. Traffic was virtually nonexistent with the occasional pedestrian walking here or there. Few of the buildings were being used professionally, that part of town being the oldest of the old in the once thriving manufacturing district.

A clean, 1961 Blue Haze Continental pulled to the curb in front of one of the better-looking buildings on the block, aside from the lower level plywood cover-ups. A man and a young boy exited the vehicle.

"Damn, that's one fine au-to-mo-bile. Sure nice of your mom to let me use it for the week."

"What is this place, Uncle Mike?" eight-year-old Lawrence questioned. "Is that named after us?" he asked as he pointed to the company logo high above, painted directly on the brick exterior and stretching across the entire front of the building from the roofline down to the top of the upper floor windows. He studied the exterior of the three-story brick building, an artifact of the industrial revolution, now crumbling, boarded up, abandoned. In truth, the building was more like five stories high. The bottom floor had double high ceilings to accommodate the machines of industry.

"You don't know? Oh, I forget how young you are," Mike said with an accent thick from a childhood on the mean streets of depression-era Chicago. He stood lanky and tall, his graying full beard and mustache hiding most of his rugged, prematurely aged face. Life for Mike had been a continuous series of missteps, horrible decisions, and unfortunate circumstances.

"Your grandfather bought this place many years ago. Your Grandma Rose probably never talks about it considering Grandpa George basically left her in Chicago to come run this place, even though she begged him not to. But that's a long story for another time. Let's just say, it killed the family, and him too, quite literally."

Mike worked the key into the lock and jostled it about until the mechanism finally gave way. He twisted the knob and pushed the door open, shining the flashlight ahead of him to guide the way. Looking back over his shoulder, he could see the hesitation in Lawrence's eyes.

"Come on boy. Ain't nothing in here to be a afraid of. I come in here all the time. It's my ... secret little hideout. You'll love it. It's a gas." In truth, Mike hadn't held down a regular job for several years and was actually living in the former office of his father - the former president of the once booming furniture store, warehouse, manufacturing facility, and company offices for The Kranski and Family Furniture Company. What little money he could muster came from selling off some of the scarce furniture pieces he dug up from the warehouse and the occasional marijuana transaction. The later only possible when he was able to afford the taxi fair to get uptown to sell to the college kids and the yuppies.

The boy's trepidation came, not from the dilapidated building, but from the man he called Uncle Mike, a man who had barely been in his life. Only recently, since the death of Lawrence's father six months prior, had Mike bothered to show his face around them, taking full advantage of the generosity of Jannie Kranski, the widow of his brother and mother to Lawrence. Jannie allowed Mike to come over for dinner a few nights a week so he would have a good, hot meal once in a while.

She knew how hard his life had been and continued to be, and Jannie could never turn her back on someone in need, especially a member of the family. Even though her deceased husband, George Jr., warned her about Mike, his criminal tendencies, and the unstable state of his mind, she ignored his past words, allowing him to be part of the family, albeit only in a small way.

Jannie had the soul of a teacher, which had been her occupation for eight years before she took a job as Assistant Administrator of the school district where they lived. That job unknowingly became paramount to their financial survival when George Jr. was killed in an automobile accident on I-90 during a snowstorm on January 3rd. The increase in salary meant the difference between selling the house and moving into rental property and staying in the home George Jr. helped build.

Another fortunate and related occurrence was the 1961 Continental, a well taken care of and classy used car bought by George Jr. and given to Jannie as a gift to celebrate her promotion. She timidly lent her cherished car to Mike so he could run errands while he babysat Lawrence. The conference in Seattle forced Jannie's hand in asking Mike for the favor of taking care of her son for the week, but she felt comfortable he wouldn't do anything stupid while she was away.

Her only concern was that he might wreck the car but she couldn't very well leave him to taxicab travel with the car sitting right there in the driveway. She gave him a stern talking-to about what she expected from him before dropping the keys in his hand, and he seemed to offer just the right amount of reciprocating concern.

"I'll be good," he said. "No messing around."

Lawrence relished the opportunity to cruise around in the blue beauty, as he referred to it, and he could no doubt use the two hundred dollars cash she offered him for watching Lawrence, not to mention the food money given to feed the two of them for the week. He took the job without hesitation, figuring he could just go about his usual business and simply lug Lawrence around with him.

Lawrence moved toward his Uncle and stayed close behind as they walked into the building, stepping carefully across the entrance hall. Their path was relatively clear of debris, though the room contained various tables and chairs, some knocked over and covered in dust, newspaper scraps and magazines, and foam coffee cups, some used, some not. To the far left side of the room rose a grand mahogany, double-wide staircase that curved in the beginning and ended parallel to the wall it was secured to.

The man and child traversed each of the thirty steps up to the second floor. They walked along the banister overlooking the entry room below, to the opposite side of the building where yet another staircase, though much smaller, took them to the third floor - originally reserved for the offices of company leadership and various white collar positions. Turning left at the top of the stairs and down a long hallway led them to the last door, a rather nondescript one if weren't for the glass emerald knob.

Lawrence marveled at the shimmering green as the flashlight illuminated the glass. Once the door was opened, natural light poured out. All the upper level windows within each office were not boarded over like they were on the first floor. There was little to no chance a person could break into the building through those windows, so there was no need.

They stepped into the room. Lawrence waited just inside as Mike walked over to the tattered mattress and box spring sitting in the corner, plopping down on the edge.

"Come on boy, nothing to be scared of in here." There were three bottles of whiskey resting next to the bed, near the wall. Mike reached down and grabbed the one closest to him, which happened to be half-empty. He unscrewed the bottle and took a swig equal to three shots. "Ah!" He coughed twice in rapid succession.

Wide-eyed, Lawrence took three steps in but stopped short of getting too close to the bed. "What is this place? It smells funny in here." He put his hand to his nose. "Do you live here?"

"I stay here sometimes, yes. It's not that bad. I got no neighbors and nobody bothers me here. It's kinda like being on a permanent camping trip - my own little survival cabin." He put finger quotes up around the word cabin.

On a chair up against the wall to Mike's right was a red duffle bag. He snatched it off the chair, unzipped it, made sure the little baggies of pot were all accounted for, took a big whiff with his face near the opening, then pulled back and zipped the bag.

"Come here and sit." Mike pounded the edge of the bed next to him. "We won't be here too long. I just needed to pick up some things."

Reluctantly, Lawrence walked over and sat on the very corner of the bed. He shifted to watch his Uncle Mike.

Mike twisted the cap from the bottle again and took a drink almost as big as the first. "You want a sip of this boy," Mike said with a sour grimace.

"It really frees up your mind."

"What is it, Uncle Mike? It smells strong."

Mike thrust the bottle in front of Lawrence. "Just try it. Take a little teeny-tiny sip. I promise you'll like it."

Lawrence did as he was told, bringing the bottle to his nose to smell it before placing it on his lips. He tipped it up slightly and let the liquid hit his tongue. Immediately, he jerked it away from his face and spit the booze onto the floor in front of him.

"I'm sorry, Uncle Mike. It's really gross. Blah." He kept licking his lips and brushing his tongue against the roof of his mouth to kill the taste.

"Ahhhh ... you're young. It grows on ya. Hang on." Mike hopped up and went to a desk in the corner of the room across from him. He pulled open the far right drawer and retrieved a Hershey's Bar. "You want this?"

The boy's eyes lit up and he nodded. "Are you sure? Mom doesn't let me eat candy." He stopped and thought about revealing something to Mike, finally deciding it was okay to tell him. "I eat butterscotch candies at my friend Aaron's house all the time. His mom keeps some in a dish by the front door. Mom doesn't know."

"Your secret is safe with me." Mike handed over the candy and Lawrence went straight to work on it, tearing off the exterior wrap before more carefully removing the inner foil.

Mike sat down again, this time much closer to Lawrence. The boy noticed but was too preoccupied to care.

"Ya know ... you can trust your Uncle Mike." He placed a hand on Lawrence's leg. "With your dad gone, you're going to need a man in your life to help mold you, make sure you grow up right."

Many months had passed since Mike's last sexual encounter, and the feel of the boy's soft flesh, even through his pants, was tantalizing and oddly erotic to him. He had never once experienced sexual arousal around a child, let alone a boy in his own family. He closed his eyes and imagined Pepper, the last women he had been with, a local prostitute he frequented, at least when money was flowing.

"Uncle Mike? What are you doing?"

Mike didn't realize that during his fantasizing, his hand had crept up the leg and inner thigh of his nephew, gently massaging his private parts.

"What?" Mike looked over to Lawrence, and upon seeing his own hand on the boy's crotch, snatched it away. "Nothing. We should probably get back to the house." He stood up, capped the bottle and returned it to the floor, then picked up his bag. "I got what I came here for. Let's go."

Lawrence sat confused but didn't think much of the grope, not fully understanding what had happened. "What about this?" He held up the wrappers of the candy.

"Just throw it on the bed." The boy complied and they left the building.

The entire ride back to the house, Mike could not stop thinking about his encounter with the boy. It spun and spun and spun around his head, like a desire for water after three days in the desert. He had urges, impulses he didn't understand and didn't really want, but he couldn't flush them from his mind.

While parked in the driveway and still sitting in the car, Mike addressed the issue with Lawrence. "Sorry about that ... touchy-feely thing back there. I was daydreaming about something else and just got carried away. We won't tell anyone about it. People might think you're weird. Agreed?"

"Oh. Okay. Can I have another chocolate bar tomorrow?"

"Sure," Mike said with enthusiasm. *This is gonna be easy*, he thought. "I'll even make sure I have some bottles of Coke up there too, so you don't have to drink that nasty whiskey. How does that sound?"

Lawrence could almost feel the sugar surging through his blood. He smiled wide and nodded with exuberance.

"All right then, let's go make some PB and J's

for lunch."

They exited the car and had a nice lunch. The incident at the furniture store was not mentioned again for the rest of the day.

***

The next morning after a restless night's sleep, Mike got out of bed and jumped in the shower. A hot shower in a clean bathroom was a luxury for Mike and he enjoyed every second of it, especially the final few minutes as he pleasured himself.

The little time he slept was filled with sexually charged dreams inspired by his encounter with Lawrence the morning before. He tried, really tried, to shake the uncomfortable feelings that developed, but he lacked the strength of moral character to leave the incident behind. He became engulfed by it.

When Lawrence shuffled into the kitchen to find his uncle drinking coffee, Mike could barely make eye contact with the boy.

Outside the kitchen window, heavy rain pelted the glass, clouds spreading a canvas that blocked out the early morning sun.

"What do you want to eat this morning?" Mike asked. He rose from his chair and went to the refrigerator, opening it to get a look at what food might be available.

"Cereal. It's in the cabinet," Lawrence responded, pointing to an area directly to Mike's left. "And orange juice."

Mike fixed Lawrence a bowl of cereal from the only box in the cabinet, and using two eight ounces glasses, poured both of them some juice. Short of getting his breakfast order, Mike and Lawrence said nothing else while in the kitchen.

With the rain still coming down in buckets at almost noon, Mike decided he needed to visit his pad in the warehouse district, if for no other reason than to grab some booze. His mind needed soothing. He was explicitly instructed by Jannie not to drink while at the house. She made it clear she did not want him intoxicated while he held responsibility for her son. He figured a few sips to take the edge off each day would be okay. Plus, it was a good excuse to get out of the house and entertain the kid and kill some time.

The two of them made fast work running to the car, getting only a little wet, the short distance keeping it to a minimum. The drive was slow, the wipers working furiously to scrap the water away. They stopped at a convenience store on the way. Lawrence stayed in the car while Mike went in to get some snacks and a coke for the boy. He came back out with a paper sack of goodies for their lunch - the supplies he might use to aid in accomplishing the bad things running through his head.

When they arrived at the warehouse, getting in without a good soaking was going to be a different story compared to at the house. They both jumped out of the car on the count of three and ran with their heads down to the main door, which had no eave above to protect from the weather. Mike had the key ready but it still took him twelve seconds to get the door open, his left hand cradling the paper sack against his body. By then, the two of them were drenched from head to toe.

They stood just inside the door, dripping wet and cold. Lawrence shook his head to shed the water from his hair. Mike used his hand to brush away the surface moisture from his arms and head.

"Let's head upstairs. I've got some towels up there we can use up to dry off. Go ahead." Mike ushered Lawrence up the stairs first. "You know where to go."

Once in the room, Mike shut the emerald-knobbed door behind them, put the bag on the bed, and found two small hand towels. He threw one over to his nephew. He then spotted the bottles sitting next to the bed and quickly snatched one up, twisting the top and tossing it across the room. He finished the booze in one shot. Instantly, his muscles relaxed, his nerves settled, and the thoughts racing through his mind slowed.

"My clothes are too wet, Uncle Mike."

"So take them off and throw them on that desk. They'll dry faster if you're not wearing them."

"I don't know." Doubt dripped from his words. "It would be weird."

"You got underwear on don't ya?"

"Yeah."

"Well, it's no different than just having swimming trunks on. You'll be fine. Here." Mike put the bottle on the floor and started to remove his shirt. "I'll take mine off too, that way it won't be so weird. Heck. It's almost like we just went for a swim anyway."

Lawrence saw logic in his Uncle's argument, so he joined Mike in stripping off his shirt, followed by his shoes, socks, and pants. They scattered their outfits across the top of the desk, leaving their shoes on the floor near its base.

They took a seat on the bed, and from the paper bag, Mike revealed a package of chocolate snack cakes, a bag of potato chips, and a glass bottle of Coke. Lawrence grew excited at the sight of the treats and quickly forgot he was sitting in his underwear next to the uncle who had touched him inappropriately on that very bed the day before.

Mike left the food alone, instead he went for another bottle of whiskey. He needed to calm his impulses. Mike forgot how fast alcohol lowered his inhibitions and often made him act irrationally. The booze was not going to help him in the way he needed.

Lawrence crunched away at the chips with gulps of Coke between. After a few minutes, he switched to the snack cakes. The sugar rushed through his veins, igniting his energy levels.

Mike just watched the boy eat and drink as he himself took sip after sip from his own bottle, each minute a step closer to oblivion.

"Where can I put these?" Lawrence asked, referring to the empty soda bottle, the snack cake packing, and the half-empty bag of chips.

Mike didn't answer immediately, trying to form words through the mental haze. "Just throw them on the floor by the door ... but off to the side." With the flick of his hand to direct the boy, he brushed the front of his own underwear, sparking his lust. With another much larger swig from the bottle, Mike went off to wonderland, hand down his underwear, completely lost to the presence of Lawrence in the room.

When the boy turned around to see his Uncle fondling himself, he froze and stayed by the door. Lawrence felt his hands shaking and put them behind his back. He wanted to speak but fear stole his vocal cords.

Mike opened his eyes and saw Lawrence trembling by the door. He refused to stop what he was doing.

"Come here boy. Sit down."

Lawrence shook his head.

"I'm not gonna hurt you. Just having a little fun."

Again, Lawrence shook his head, this time with vigor. He turned slightly and put a hand on the doorknob, ready to run out of the room. He wanted no part of his Uncle Mike's behavior.

When Mike saw the boy's move to leave the room, he pulled his hand away from his crotch and slipped it between the mattress and the box spring, revealing a switch blade. He pressed the button and out popped the five-inch blade.

"I want to go home," Lawrence sobbed, tears erupting.

"Get your fuckin' hand off that knob boy, or I'll use this blade to take some of the fingers off of it. Do it now!"

The boy had never seen that side of his uncle. Too scared to defy him, Lawrence did as he was instructed and continued to cry. He wished he had run away. After that day, he wished for many things to be different.

12

Saturday, November 10th, 2012 – 8:38 a.m.
Unknown Location

Cole peeled his eyes back, groggy, his body heavy. He brought his left hand to the side of his neck in response to a pain that suddenly appeared. His index finger brushed across a small bump. He picked at it until the scab came off onto his finger. He looked at it for a second before flicking it to the floor. He touched the tiny wound again. No blood. Something had pricked him. He blew it off, more concerned about the task ahead of him.

As his senses returned, the cold air of the room smacked him in the face. His nose had lost sensation from being exposed to the bitter chill for so many hours. He cupped his hand around his nose, lips, and chin until they warmed up.

He looked to the clock and assumed only a few hours had passed. He wondered how much longer he could tolerate the room with no heat.

He stayed relatively calm considering the circumstances. *I suppose I shouldn't be surprised how well I'm handling this crap. Locked in a room by some psycho bastard. Been there, done that. Alone ... cold ... no future. Check. Check. Check.*

I just wish I knew who was doing this to me. I could think of quite a few people that might still be raw about the past, especially if they know the truth of my choices. Two kids died because of me and I lived. My tortured existence, my pitiful excuse for a life, this room. They're probably mild compared to what I deserve. Maybe I should just give up. Maybe I just don't care.

His hunger and thirst and caffeine headache drew him up from the bed, ready to finish off the water he had saved from earlier. He threw his legs off the cot and noticed that something in the middle of the room was different. The cup he had left under the cot had now returned to the middle of the floor but it wasn't alone. Another envelope sat next to it, and behind them, an additional small area of the floor had been cleared of keys.

"How the hell did someone sneak in here while I was asleep and not wake me up?" He puzzled over the idea for a minute when he remembered the tiny wound he discovered on his neck. "I see. So, gassing me wasn't enough, now you're going to drug me too. Well played. Not that I really giiiiiiive ... aaaaaaa ... shiiiiiiiit!"

Cole got to his feet and leered at the small window on the wall across from him, believing someone was behind it and had been the whole time, watching him.

"Whoever you are, I'm losing interest in this little game of yours. If you're going to kill me, why not just do it and be done with it? Whatever you think I did, I admit it. I'm a horrible fucking human being who made a very bad mistake when he was a kid. So, go ahead! End it! Fucking end it!"

He plopped back down, out of breath, practically foaming at the mouth. The envelope on the floor started to bug him. Thoughts of what might be inside itched at his brain and his psyche. He also thought about saying the hell with it and just lying back down, but a small part of him was curious and wanted to be engaged in whatever his captor's end game would be.

He decided to continue, if only because he felt he owed it to Justin and Kylie, but certainly not for the entertainment of a faceless villain.

He inhaled deeply and exhaled with the same intensity before rising up, stepping over to pick up the envelope and the cup, and settling back down on the cot. He was happy to discover the cup was again full, so he drank half the liquid, knowing there was no point in saving any. He didn't intend to be there much longer, one way or another.

He put the cup on the floor under the cot again and took his first look at the front of his next clue.

☐

Every assist comes with a price
This one costs you:
(FIRE - FOOD - WATER - LIFE)
3 . . .

As before, written in red marker, the envelope read: Every assist comes with a price. This one costs you: (HEAT, FOOD, WATER, LIFE) 3...

There was a red X over the words heat and food. Cole assumed that would be the case since only the water was left and there was no bowl. *Doesn't take a genius to figure out this crap.*

Cole flipped the envelope over, opened it up, and pulled out the usual the bi-folded piece of paper. Dread flashed across his face at the sight of a black and white image on the paper, an image of a dark room with two children on twin mattresses, both cuffed to a metal grate behind them. The two children were unknown to him but he did not see their real faces. His mind supplanted Justin and Kylie's in their place.

He looked away from the photo and truly started to hate the person who put him in the room full of keys. He closed his eyes and tipped is head halfway back. The guilt he had been experiencing for twenty years rose again. A lump in his throat made it hard to swallow. He sniffed, on the verge of tears, but he held them back.

"I'm sorry. I'm sorry. I'm sorry. What else will you have me to do to express that." Cole pulled his head back down and opened his eyes to the photo. Through the thin paper, he saw fragments of words in black ink behind the photo.

He unfolded the copy paper to discover another clue printed on the inside, as if the photo was the greeting card front. It read: blacK is the keY to your escape. seems alL too famIliar. onE gets out but the Duo remaIn. will that bE your Decision again? Watch the clock ... tick.

blacK is the keY to your escape. seems alL too

famIliar. onE gets out but the Duo remaIn.

will that bE your Decision again?

Watch the clock ... tick.

Cole ignored the hidden words – KYLIE DIED - within the message, confused about one line in particular: Will that be your decision again?

"What the hell does that mean? What decision?" He rubbed the right side of his head to try and relieve his headache, and maybe to jog his brain into figuring out the meaning behind the latest note.

"I'm too tired and cold and in pain. Please end this. I just don't want to do this anymore."

He closed the paper and looked to the image again. This time, he saw the two children for who they really were, not as Justin and Kylie, and he finally understood what the decision was he would have to make. The bastard responsible was holding two children somewhere nearby and it would be up to Cole to rescue them. *Clever.*

He wondered if saving the two kids would really be a chance to redeem himself or if the entire thing was some elaborate setup to entertain the mind of a madman, with no real hope existing at all. He doubted this trial would make him feel any different, knowing that no matter what he did, he could not go back and fix his prior mistakes. *Do good deeds in the present conquer a man's past indiscretions? If so, how many is enough? How many demons must be slain before the gates of hell are closed for good?*

As Cole thought about where the children in the photo might be, the first words of the most recent clue popped into his head: Black is the key for you.

"Black is the key. I suppose he could mean that literally, as in, the key I need is black. His eyes darted around the floor of the room, focusing on the skeletons keys. There were a few different colors amongst them, black being one. He quickly realized there weren't actually that many black ones that would fit in the door, so sorting them out and discovering the right one should be easy.

From his earlier water drinking and the constant fight to stay warm, his bladder went from nothing to urgent. He loathed the idea of using the bucket, as he had no idea how the smell would affect the room. Then again, his revelation about the black key might mean his time in the room was coming to an end.

No longer able to wait, he dropped the letter

and the envelope, quickly stepped over to the bucket, and relieved himself. As bad as the impulse to go was, he was surprised at how fast the stream trickled down to nothing. He did feel better though.

When he turned around, the new area in the middle of the floor that had been cleared while he was unconscious revealed something to him, something he was amazed he hadn't seen when he picked up the cup and the envelope. On the concrete were three blue arrows made from painter's tape, all pointing toward the wall with the small window.

"Jesus, I really need to pay better attention. How the hell could I miss that? Not that I know what it means."

No sooner had the words escaped his lips, the sound of metal scraping came from the window wall, startling Cole. An orange glow appeared in the glass that was not there before.

He walked over to the window, his suspicions and curiosity piqued. Leery of what he might find, Cole put his hands on the wall and drew his face to the glass.

The room next door was dark, a soft yellow-orange light bulb dangled from the center of the ceiling. Without being sure of his depth perception as he looked through the tinted glass and the shadows, Cole guessed the room was about four times the size of his own cell. The edges and corners of the room were totally black. The light from the single bulb could only reach so far.

The side wall straight across from him was the only thing he needed to see. There were two old, ragged mattresses on the floor and up against the wall, and on them, two young children chained to a metal grate.

Cole's bottom lip quivered. He wondered if he was really still alive or just dead and suffering through a form of purgatory. He shook off the idea. Based on the clues he had been given, Cole knew exactly what he needed to do.

"You can't be serious? What kind of scumbag are you? I suppose I already know the answer to that."

Cole whipped around and browsed the floor with his eyes once again looking for black skeleton keys. As he discovered before, there weren't many, which relieved him. He had no idea how much time he had left. The last envelope had a three on it. *Countdown to zero. I'm sure there will be more surprises around the corner, but you can do this. Just focus on the task at hand and take each challenge one at a time. I'll get the kids out, then go from there.*

He went to work on gathering the possible keys, placing them on the cot. Ten minutes passed before he finished and was ready to start trying the keys. Even in the chill of the room, he worked up a mild sweat, so he sipped on some water before grabbing the first five keys. Without actually counting, Cole figured there were forty to fifty of them.

"This shouldn't take long."

One at a time, he checked and double-checked each key, tossing the bad ones onto the floor with a flick of his wrist. Only his fourth handful in, the final key from that group went in the lock, two revolutions to the right, click.

His eyes widened, his heart raced. The time had come to exit his prison and let the next phase begin. He removed the key and stuffed it in his pocket.

Cole was ready to pull the handle but was terrified at what he might find on the other side. He shivered, maybe from the fear, maybe from the cold, but either way, it made him think of his jacket. He put it on and returned to the door, hand at the ready. He gripped the handle tight and pulled as slow as he could. As he did, the shield covering the little window slammed shut, making Cole jump. He continued. Once he had pulled the door halfway open, the light bulb in his room grew bright and intense, then popped and sizzled to blackness.

13

Monday, November 9th, 1992 – 10:27 a.m.
Lansing, Michigan

"This is Detective Jebsen. What can I do for you?" he asked after picking up the phone from his desk at the police department. He had a corner office with one little window. The room was neat and tidy, every book in its place, every folder neatly stacked. The desk itself, on the other hand, was another matter entirely. While he worked on cases, the papers and folders scattered across the surface were piles and piles of chaos and reckless abandon. He preferred the mess for his active cases. He viewed them as puzzles that needed to be solved, so if everything was neat and looked ready to be filed, that must mean the puzzle was done.

"Hi, Jeb. It's Beth. Got something for ya."

"Oh. Let me have it. Good news I hope."

"That's for you to decide. For the skeleton, cause of death is inconclusive. As best as we can determine, the person died in the fire. We found no other evidence to support death beforehand."

"Well, that's something I guess. Just not too helpful to the investigation. Anything else?"

"Oh yeah. And here is where it gets interesting. We found partial skeletal remains from a completely different person, definitely a child, and even with what little we have, determined it was likely from someone a little older than the full set."

"Sex?" Jeb asked, theories pulsing through his brain.

"Can't tell."

"Damn. But one is discernibly larger than the other?"

"Yes. If I had to guess, the skeleton is from an eight-year-old child, the partial bones from a ten or eleven-year-old."

"That fits the description of Kylie and Justin exactly."

"Speaking of, I got a fax coming in right now. Might be the dental records I was waiting on. Hang on just a second."

Beth put the phone down and hustled to the

fax machine to retrieve the sheet of paper sent by the laboratory in town they hired for dental matching work. She returned quickly to the phone and picked it up.

"Jeb."

"Yeah."

"We have a match. The skeleton is positively identified as Kylie Simpson.

"Well, shit." Jeb let out a big sigh. "Shit! Shit! Shit!" Jeb slammed the phone on his desk each time he said the word. "Thanks, Beth. I gotta go. Sorry about that."

Jeb didn't even give her time to respond, he just ended the phone call. His focus turned entirely to Cole and determining how he might get answers from the boy. Unscrupulous thoughts entered his mind. He wanted the psycho off the streets and Cole was there best and last chance to help with that. The boy needed to open up or the lives of other children might be at risk.

From out of the bullpen, Detective Pagano popped his head into Jeb's office. "Hey Jeb, got some info on the Redman case. We found the property owners."

Jeb waved him in. "What you got?"

"An Alfred Jones, who's been living in the Tampa Bay Area in Florida for the past fourteen years, owns the property. Records show it's been in his family for generations. I talked to him this morning and he said no one in his family, including himself, had been to the property in close to five years. He's retired and they no longer have any family up here to visit. He suggested someone may have been squatting at the cabin. His alibi checks out."

"Crap. What about neighbors? Certainly, somebody must have seen a vehicle coming and going from the property. People are nosy."

"Dead end. The neighbor to the west is the one that reported the fire, a Shirley Henderson, fifty-nine-year-old widow. She said she saw smoke coming from that area when she woke up, around 6:30 a.m., but didn't think much of it. A few hours later, the smoke was still going, and she didn't think anyone used the property anymore, so as a precaution, she went ahead and called the fire department. She knows the Jones' too. She verified his story about not being here in many years. They had dinner three nights before the Jones' moved to Florida and she said they had only been back once, that she knew of - about five years ago."

"Double crap." Jeb's mind bounced a few ideas around. "And this Jones guy is sure he has no family up here that might know about the cabin? Any friends?"

"He seemed pretty confident, but over the

many years his family lived in this area, he said there were hundreds of people, if not thousands that knew about the property, and he had no way of narrowing that down."

"Yeah, I suppose not. Damn it! That is a serious wrinkle. Well, thanks for the update. Oh yeah, before I forget. I just talked to Beth. The skeleton found at the cabin has been positively identified through dental records as Kylie Simpson."

"No shit! There's no way that Redman boy isn't connected to this. Anything else?"

"Yep. More bones from another person were found as well, not enough to make an I.D. though. Definitely from a child a little older than Kylie."

"That's not good."

"No, it's not. Looks like we got a double homicide and a giant fucking brick wall in front of us. Hopefully Cole Redman is a little more forthcoming this afternoon when I question him."

"I hope so. This case is quickly gettin' icy."

Jeb nodded as he racked his brain for ideas on ways to open Cole up. None of them were good ones.

Three hours, forty-one minutes later -

The sun had popped out early and stayed out. The high temperature for the day was forecast at just thirty-eight degrees but the solar warmth gave the illusion of near fifty. When Detective Jebsen and Dr. Weinstein exited Jeb's car at the curb of the Redman residence, Jeb felt too hot to leave his suit coat on. He pulled the notebook and pen from the inside pocket and tossed the jacket in the back seat.

"This is turning out to be a gorgeous day," Dr. Weinstein said. She inhaled a big, slow breath through her nose, enjoying every bit of the clean and crisp late fall air.

"Yeah. I was roasting in that damn thing."

They walked side by side until they reached the sidewalk leading to the front porch, then Jeb took the lead.

"You think there's any chance Cole will have more to say?" Dr. Weinstein asked.

"I doubt it, but even if he does, not sure how much help it will be, now that we know the other two are dead. I'm sure whoever the fucker is that did this is long gone."

"You never know. Maybe we got a careless psycho here. Wouldn't be the first time."

They arrived at the front door of the quaint, single-story house. The red door was perfectly centered between two double windows on the front of the house. The exterior had been updated with white vinyl siding and a black asphalt roof, but the windows and door were original from the late sixties, best as they could tell.

Jeb shrugged his shoulders in response to the doctor's comments before pushing the doorbell. He thought about it for a moment, then decided to rap three times on the door as well.

Dr. Weinstein moved to a position at Jeb's side but still partially behind him.

Gretchen opened the door. "Hello, Detective Jebsen." Gretchen turned and nodded to the doctor. "Dr. Weinstein. Please come in." She stepped aside and allowed them both to enter the living room, a small space that didn't allow for much furniture.

The couch at the front window was old and somewhere between gold and mustard. Near the side window was a bonded leather recliner, burgundy in color that had seen better days. The only other furniture in the room were a matching oak end table and coffee table, and a similarly styled but not matching television stand with a nineteen-inch Sony Trinitron TV and Magnavox VCR.

"Please sit down," Gretchen said as she guided them to the couch.

"Thank you, Ms. Redman, for seeing us again. How is Cole doing?" Jeb asked. Dr. Weinstein sat on the couch, nearest the door, Jeb on the other end.

"You can ask him yourself." Gretchen was courteous but firm. Her displeasure with the questioning of her son the day before still festered within, though the affects had worn some. "Cole! Can you please come in here?" She smiled and turned to the tiny hallway leading to the kitchen, bath, and the two bedrooms of the home. Cole emerged from the dark and slipped under his mother's left arm.

"Hello, Cole," Jeb said.

Gretchen looked down to her son. "Detective Jebsen would like to ask you few more questions. Help them out and you can go back to reading. I'm sure it will be quick." She directed the last part dead into the eyes of Jeb, who nodded in return.

"But mom, I don't really want to."

"You have to. But I promise you, this will be the last time. So, go ahead. I'll be right in the kitchen." She bent over, softly grabbed Cole's right cheek between the thumb and index finger of her left hand, and kissed him on the forehead. "Just be honest and do the best you can and it will be over before you know it."

Cole offered a reluctant smile. He knew his mother would never put him in danger or intentionally let anyone hurt him. "Okay. I'll try."

He lied. He had no intentions of trying. He intended to hide the whole truth, again. He had an entire day to steel his nerve and rehearse the story he had already told, should he ever need to tell it again. Now, it was just a matter of repeating it. He was not going to invite the devil back into his life, no matter the consequences, that much he was certain of.

He dreamt of Justin and Kylie, the dark room, the emerald knob, and they were not nightmares. In the dream, Justin and Kylie ran alongside him from the cabin and through the woods. They all shared a room at the hospital where they comforted each other about the horrible things that had been done them, and cried together as the fear they had experienced left forever when the news came about how the police had captured the bad man and taken him to prison - forever.

Cole's brain played false memories in his sleep, ones of horsing around on the playground at school with his new best friends, the brother and sister pair that helped him cope with their shared nightmare. They smiled and laughed as the merry-go-round spun and spun until they all jumped off, running and falling dizzy into the grass.

Sleep was a happy time for Cole on that night. It was only when he awoke that reality slapped him in the face again. The police arriving at his house for another round of questioning might as well have been someone punching him in the gut. His stomach churned with fear.

Cole walked over and sat down in the recliner. Gretchen left the room. Jeb and Dr. Weinstein shifted in their seats to face Cole more directly.

"How ya feeling bud?" Jeb asked.

"Okay, I guess, Detective." Cole looked to Jeb then looked down quickly, his eyes darting up and down every four or five seconds, scared to make permanent eye contact.

"We don't have to be so formal. You can call me Jeb. You remember Dr. Weinstein?"

Cole nodded.

The doctor smiled. "Hello, Cole. Glad to see you're doing well."

Cole nodded again without looking to her.

Detective Jebsen dove right in. "So, can you remember anything new about what happened to you? Where you might have been or who might have taken you?"

Cole puzzled over a response then simply shook his head.

"You sure? Remember, even the smallest detail could help us out. Smells, sounds, anything like that?"

"I really can't remember anything. I don't know where I was. When I woke up, I just ran.

Next thing I knew, I was in the hospital." Cole closed his eyes for a moment but opened them quickly when the face of his tormentor appeared.

Jeb felt the truth was hiding somewhere and that Cole remembered a hell of a lot more than he was sharing. It frustrated him. His mind searched for a way to break through. He didn't doubt that Cole couldn't remember everything, but Jeb could see the pain and fear in Cole's eyes, the proverbial windows to the soul, and he knew there was more to be said, if only the child would open up.

If there was one thing Jeb understood from his years on the job, it was that people are much less afraid of scary events than they are of scary people. Scary events come and go, they happen, they hurt, but they can't come back. Scary people, on the other hand, can come back. They will haunt you. When he looked into Cole's eyes, the dread hiding there was not for some horrible experience. Cole feared another human being - that much was obvious. There was someone out there that could hurt him again.

With a dead-end in sight, Jeb took one last leap to break Cole open, even though it was equally likely to shut him down. *What other choice do I have? I need more. This case is going to come to a screeching fuckin' halt if this kid doesn't give me something.*

"I thought I'd let you know, we had a break in the case of those two other missing children I was telling you about yesterday - Justin and Kylie Simpson."

Cole's eyes lit up. Terror welled up from his bones to his skin. He suddenly realized his reaction was too obvious, so he brought his facial expression back to a more neutral state. Even as quick as the reaction came and went, Jeb and Emma noticed.

"This information hasn't been released to the public yet but ... we found a cabin out in the woods not far from where *you* were found."

The acid in Cole's stomach bubbled and his hands began to shake lightly.

"And do you know what we found out there?"

Dr. Weinstein tapped the elbow of Jeb, who turned his head. The doctor furrowed her brow and gave him a facial expression that begged the question: what the hell are you doing?

He turned back to Cole, ignoring her concern. "Any idea?"

"No," Cole mustered with a creaky voice.

"We found the place burnt to the ground ... and inside, the bones of a little girl just identified with dental records as Kylie Simpson. There were a few other bones from another child, as yet identified. We assume they are from her brother."

"Detective Jebsen?"

Jeb went on, continuing to ignore Emma. "You sure you don't know anything about that? Out in the woods, away from people and buildings? She was chained to a bed." Jeb increased the volume and intensity of his voice. "There were two other chains Cole. One for Justin ... and one for you. Am I right? Tell me I'm lying!" He had never lost his mind during questioning like that before, least of all with a child. He wanted answers. No. He needed answers. He being so close to valuable information, seeing the shadow of it through the frosted glass case known as Cole Redman and not being able to bring it into focus, put Jeb over the edge. Maybe it was the fact Detective Jebsen had two kids of his own, both younger than Kylie, that made the case more real to him. Maybe it was just the detective in him who didn't like cases bound for the cold stack. Either way, he crossed a line.

"Detective Jebsen! That is enough!" Emma stood up.

From the kitchen, Gretchen could hear the raised voices. She dropped the sponge she was using to wipe the counter and bolted for the living room.

Cole started to cry. "I don't know anything."

His words were interrupted by Dr. Weinstein. "Cole, you don't have to say anymore. As Child

Advocate, I'm ending this interview."

Jeb stood up to try and intimidate Cole. "You remember his face, don't you, Cole? You dream about it. I know you do. Just tell us what he looked like," he ordered.

"As his mother, *I'm* ending this interview. Detective Jebsen, please leave this house immediately."

"Jeb, let's go," Emma commanded. She turned to Gretchen. "I'm terribly sorry, Ms. Redman. We're leaving."

"Damn it! There are two dead children out there and we don't have the first clue as to who did it."

"I don't really care," Gretchen barked.

"He could be out there right now, doing this to other kids and your son knows something. Don't you see how important this is? He's just scared."

"Detective! Don't make me ask again! I don't want to get nasty." Gretchen made eye contact with Cole. "Come here baby."

Cole stood up, slow, and put a hand on his stomach. "I think I'm going to throw up." He carefully exhaled, trying as hard as he could to hold it down.

"Run to bathroom baby. Use the toilet, not the sink, if you need to."

Cole walked fast across the room and behind

his mother, disappearing into the black of the hall. He entered the bathroom, slamming the door shut behind him. He fell to his knees at the base of the toilet just in time to release.

"We need to leave, Jeb," Emma said.

Gretchen marched to the front door, aggressively opened it, and held the knob tight with rage. "If you please. And don't bother coming back."

Jeb motioned for Emma to walk ahead of him. She did and he followed, stopping in front of Gretchen.

"This is a big mistake," Jeb said, then he turned away and left the house, meeting Dr. Weinstein on the sidewalk. He jumped at the sound of the front door slamming shut.

Inside, Gretchen leaned against the door and put her hands to her face in frustration. She took several deep breaths to try and calm her nerves.

"Uhhh ... the audacity." She suddenly remembered Cole was sick in the bathroom, so she rushed to see him.

She gently knocked on the door and entered to find Cole rinsing is mouth at the sink. She rubbed the top and back of his head. "You okay sweetie? They're gone and you won't have to see them ever again."

Cole swished the water in his mouth and spit it out. "Better." He spun around to face his mother.

"You need to go lay down? Take a nap?"

Cole nodded. Gretchen pulled him close and hugged him tight. He almost cried again but held it back. She kissed the top of his head and ushered him to his room.

Once under the covers, she tucked him in and kissed him again, this time on the forehead.

"I'll check on you in a little while. Just try and rest, even if you can't sleep."

Cole closed his eyes. Gretchen just stared at him for minute before exiting the room, flicking the light switch and closing the door as she left.

Inside the car, Jeb put the key in the ignition but didn't immediately turn it.

"What the hell was that all about, Jeb? Jesus!" Emma shifted her body to face him.

He exhaled loudly and shook his head. He gathered his thoughts before answering. "I had to take a chance. Other lives might be at stake."

"Not like that you didn't. You broke just about every protocol we have for questioning kids, Jeb. You just can't do shit like that. You may have jeopardized any future chance we had of getting information out of him. No matter what, you're not going to be able to get within ten feet of him now. Tell me, how's that going to help?" She shook her head in disgust.

"Intel given to us a year from now isn't gonna do us any damn good and you know it. We whiffed on this one, big time." Jeb finally turned the key and put the shifter into drive. "Somewhere out there, a bat-shit crazy kid killer is looking for more, and I hate to think of what he did before he burned their bodies. Doesn't that bother you?" Jeb checked his side mirror and pulled onto the quiet street.

Emma shifted back properly in her seat. "Of course it bothers me, but as professionals, our integrity must remain no matter how difficult the challenge or we become the very thing we work so hard to reign in - heartless, lacking empathy, or in simplistic terms, bad human beings. That's not you Jeb. That's not you."

She was right and he knew it. They remained silent for the rest of the drive back to the station.

Jeb decided that if he could do it all over again, nothing would change, but he wasn't heartless. Cole reminded him of an older version of his own son, so the problem might have been found in his inability to set aside his emotions. He couldn't remember a case that tugged at his soul like that one had, but then again, cases of child abduction and murder didn't happen every day in west Michigan. *Thank god for that*, he thought.

As they all feared, the case ran cold after that.

No further evidence could be found at the sight of the burned down cabin, Cole was never questioned again by the police, and the perpetrator of a kidnapping and murder of two children was never found. The community only hoped that whomever the monster was, they had moved on from the area, never to return. They hoped.

About a year later -

As Cole had requested the week before, Gretchen picked him up from school and drove him to the cemetery. The two children from his school killed the year before were buried there. She remembered to bring the potted planted from his room, the Red Trillium she had bought for him the previous summer.

When they arrived at the Pleasant Hill Cemetery and pulled to the end of a long, winding road covered in giant, red, orange, and brown leaves, Gretchen stopped.

"You sure you want to go by yourself?" Gretchen asked.

"Yes, mom." Cole held the pot in his lap. He pulled the door handle and swung his legs out.

"I love you baby. I'll be here waiting for you."

Cole didn't respond. He left the car, walking in front of it on his way to the northwest corner of the cemetery. The branches of a large willow tree draped down above the two grave markers. Most of the leaves had fallen.

He stared at the tree behind the markers instead of the markers themselves. He couldn't bear to look at them. His eyes glanced down, then he closed them just as fast.

He had practiced the words he intended to say to them for weeks, but as he stood there, he failed to remember a single one. The chilly air and his desire for a hot dinner urged him to say something. He improvised.

"I'm sorry you died." A flood of images from the night of his escape raced through his memory like a blur of fast moving cars on the racetrack. So intense were the memories, he fell to his knees and almost dropped the plant. He didn't cry, but instead grew terrified.

Already anxious to leave, he plucked two red leaves from one of the stems and placed one at the base of each grave marker. He pulled the third leaf off the stem and just looked at it, clueless as to what to do with the one that represented himself. Unsure why, Cole inserted the leaf into his mouth and chewed it, even though the bitter taste. Once he couldn't stand it anymore, he swallowed.

He set the pot on the ground, stood up, brushed the dirt from his knees, and picked the pot back up.

"Please forgive me," Cole whispered as if someone was nearby and he didn't want them to hear. He turned and ran back to the car, anxious to get away from his loathing, his past, his demons.

He got in the car and slammed the door shut.

"Everything okay, Cole? Your knees are covered in dirt."

"Fine. Can we please just go home." His hands were trembling. Gretchen noticed.

"Okay sweetie. I bet you're hungry. It's grilled cheese and tomato soup tonight."

Cole nodded but he didn't need to be told. He always remembered grilled cheese night. It was his favorite. It was the only other thing he thought about the entire day. The meal would comfort him, at least until he fell asleep, but there was nothing that could placate his dream world. He would sit awake in his bed for hours trying to resist falling asleep but only until his eyelids became like lead weights that were bound to sink.

14

Saturday, November 10th, 2012 – 10:01 a.m.
Unknown Location

His eyes took a minute to adjust to the blackness of the hallway. Cole decided to leave the door ajar behind him as a reference point, just in case he got confused about his location within the building. Once his eyes dilated to a size making it possible for him to see a few feet in front of him, he surveyed his surroundings.

The hallway was much like his room, solemn and gray, only not as cold. Out of habit, he put a hand around the key dangling from his neck, much like if it were a crucifix or a set of rosary beads. He wanted out. He wanted the children out. He wished for success in both.

To his right, he could see the faintest glow of pink coming from around a corner at the end of the twenty-five-foot-long hallway. The path to that light was dim. To his left, total darkness.

Cole had no idea what he might find to the right, and though he had no doubt the left had secrets waiting to be discovered, it also held a room with two children.

He pondered the idea of getting out, going for help, and coming back to rescue the children, or at least allowing the authorities to do so. The game being orchestrated, however, was not lost on Cole. *Will this guy just kill the kids if I leave? Most likely. Damn it! If I go after them, will he kill me and them?*

For a moment, the fear overtook him. He turned to the right, put his left hand on the wall across from the room he exited, and started walking, fast, using the wall as a guide. Visibility increased with each step toward the glow. The light evolved from pink to neon red as he approached.

At the corner of the hallway, he turned left, and to his surprise, just five feet in front of him was a painted white metal door with an exit sign hanging above, shining like a beacon to freedom.

He stepped forward, closed his eyes, and put a

hopeful grasp around the brass knob. Slowly, he opened his eyes and began to twist the knob. Before turning even an inch, he spotted something unusual on the door. Secured with a thin strip of painter's tape was a book of matches. He knew what they were for. His captor knew he would run out. Cole let go the knob.

"I guess I'm perfectly predictable. And still a big chicken shit." He sighed. "Cole, it's time face your fate. You haven't spent the last twenty years in a living hell to end up making the same stupid decisions all over again. Time to grow a pair."

Cole ripped the tape from the door and let the matches fall into his hand. He stared at the match book. e knew what he needed to do but the courage to do it remained aloof.

"You're a grown man, Cole, not an eleven-year-old boy. It's not that complicated. Go save those damn kids. If all else fails, at least you'll die knowing you made a better choice this time."

With tentative steps, Cole walked back down the hallway - the room next to his own the destination. He was glad to find the door to his room still open but he walked right past it. Twelve feet on, he discovered a steel door, cold to the touch. Using the fingers of his right hand, he inspected the right-center of the door and discovered what he believed to be a glass knob with a large keyhole a few inches beneath it. As quiet as possible, he twisted the knob and pushed. The door was locked.

To get a better look at the door in front of him, he decided to use the matches provided to him, likely intended for this exact purpose. Cole ripped a match free from the book and folded back the flap. He struck the match between the flap and the striking strip, creating a small flame that grew quickly.

Cole held the match eighteen inches from his face and saw the manila envelope floating on the surface of the door. He read the words written in the usual red marker: Every assist comes with a price. This one costs you: (HEAT, FOOD, WATER, LIFE) 2 ...

The words heat, food, and water were crossed out.

"Obviously," Cole said as he rolled his eyes. He glanced down and saw a plastic cup sitting on the ground, similar to the one from his room. He tapped it with his foot and it fell over, empty. He shook his head, beginning to view the entire game as stupid and juvenile.

He flinched when the flame from his match hit his fingertips, causing him to drop it. It smoldered quickly. He struck another and removed the envelope from the door, finding the blue tape again, folded backward on itself to create a double-sided loop used to secure it to the door.

"Let's get this over with." He thought about how he would open the clasp with only one hand available, so he dropped the match.

Once again in the dark, he opened the envelope and inserted his hand. He could feel the usual piece of paper, but at the bottom sat something new. With his index finger, he slid the small metal object up the inside of the envelope, using his thumb to help secure it. The object was a small key. He had no idea what it was for. Briefly, he thought it might be for the door in front of him, but it seemed too small for such a large keyhole. He placed it in his right, front pants pocket for safekeeping, then pulled the paper from the envelope, placing it between his lips to secure it and free up his hands.

He dropped the envelope off to his side and once again struck a match, holding it with his right hand and using his left to remove the paper from his mouth. The note had the usual clue with a message imbedded: only you hold the key to theIr fReedom and you'vE had it all along. will you save theM or sAve yourself? the exIt is straight dowN thE hall. deciDe. The clock has stopped.

only you hold the key to theIr fReedom and you'vE had

it all along. will you save theM or sAve yourself?

the exIt is straight dowN thE hall. deciDe.

The clock has stopped.

The words - I REMAINED - stood out from the clue. Cole had his suspicions about the culprit behind the game. He hoped he was wrong. He tossed the match and dropped the note.

"I've had it all along?" Unconsciously, he grabbed the key hanging around his neck, rubbing it between his fingers as he stood in the pitch black. It helped him think. He stopped abruptly. "Well, no shit. This key? How is that possible?"

He pulled the necklace over his head and left it hanging from his wrist as he lit another match. Cole moved his hand around with the flame to get a better look at the door. The glimmer of the emerald knob caught his attention.

"How the hell did I not notice that before?"

He continued to scan the door. Suddenly, the memories of his childhood escape came flooding back. The door before him was the same door he escaped through at the cabin twenty years earlier. The large steel rivets, the rust streaks, the green glass knob, all virtually unchanged. He could not conceive of how someone could perfectly recreate it. It was exactly the same. *This is not possible. That cabin burned to the ground. How is this door here? Did he remove it before burning that place down? Why would he do that?*

There was only one way to know for sure, so he let the necklace slide to his left hand, and with the flame getting close to his fingertips again, he inserted the key in the door, the same key he long held both sacred and cursed.

The key represented a constant reminder of his choice to lie, a choice that he knew resulted in the death of two children from his school, two children that became kindred spirits with his own soul. The guilt of his choice to hide the truth, and the fact that he survived and they did not, remained seared into that key. It burned his soul every day since. He felt he deserved it, and maybe he did.

Cole turned the key and heard the lock scrap and click. After dropping the match, he removed the key and returned the necklace to its proper place. Ready to take on whatever nightmare might lie ahead, he put his hand on the knob, twisted to the left, and pushed the door open.

The room, though similar to the one he was held captive in with the same orange glow from the single bulb and floor to ceiling cold concrete, was indeed much larger. The light did not extend to the corners or edges. To Cole's left, he could see the tiny window he had looked through earlier. On the right side, directly in the middle of the wall, were the two twin-sized mattresses, both without box springs and sitting directly on the floor. Behind the mattresses was a section of wrought-iron fencing, four-feet tall by eight-feet wide, secured to the wall and floor with large bolts.

Two children, a boy of ten or eleven years old and a girl of eight, as far as Cole could tell, laid separately on different mattresses, each with a handcuff around one wrist, the other end attached to the fence behind. Even in the faint light, Cole could see they were filthy, cold, and traumatized. He couldn't help but once again see

Justin and Kylie in their pitiful and starving faces.

I'm growing tired of this sick game. Very, very tired.

Cole closed his eyes for a few seconds to gather his thoughts. He remembered the key in his pocket from the envelope and removed it. Without enough light to tell for sure, he assumed the key was made for the cuffs. It seemed like the right size. He doubted it would be that easy.

Cole hustled over to the children, figuring if he could spring them free and get them out of the building quickly, he would feel better knowing they were safe, even if ultimately, he did not get to join them.

The children were awake but lethargic, perhaps even drugged. They didn't even react to Cole's presence. He went to work immediately on the cuff around the wrist of the little girl - blonde, innocent. His hand shook terribly as he fit the key in the cuff. He turned it and released the cold, metal grip of the ring. She did not move. Working fast, he stepped over to the other side of the beds, knelt down, and did the same for the boy.

Gently, he shook the boy's arm to alert him. "Are you okay?" Cole whispered. "We need to get you two out of here?"

The boy opened his eyes ever so slightly but said nothing.

"Hey. Can you get up?" Cole kept his voice

down.

The boy slowly brought his arm from the bed as if it weighed fifty pounds, raising his index finger a little. With a breathy and struggling voice, the boy said, "He's here." His arm collapsed. Even with the cuffs removed, the children were in no condition, physically or mentally, to leave the room on their own.

From the corner of the room, farthest from the door and opposite the kids, came a slow and deliberate clap. Clap. Clap. Clap. Clap.

Cole's heart skipped a beat as he whipped around, eyes locked on the corner, shadow hiding the source of the clap. He was undecided about whether he wanted to just grab the kids and bolt or stick around and find out who the bastard hiding in the dark was.

"Well done," the man from the shadows spoke. "I was absolutely convinced that you would do today, exactly what you did twenty years ago - run away and leave the others behind. And by the way, if you're thinking about running, don't bother." A gun cocked. "You might not be able to see me, but I can see you just fine."

"Why are you doing this? Why the kids? If you wanted me, why didn't you just grab *me*?" Before he entered the room, Cole believed he was dealing with the same man responsible for taking him as a child, but he was sure he would remember the sound of his voice, even after twenty years. His dreams still echoed with that deep, aggressive rasp. This person hiding in the shadows sounded nothing like his original tormentor.

"I had to see what kind of man you had become. Clearly, you are exceeding my expectations. When you reached the exit door, I was sure as shit you were out of here, but you surprised me."

"Oh, you'll find I'm full of surprises." He regretted the words the moment they left his mouth. *What the hell are you doing Cole? This is no time to be smug.* "So, tell me, is that exit door unlocked?" Cole asked, quickly changing the subject.

"Oh, yes. Like you did twenty years ago, you could have run away, scared and spineless and left these two behind. You never forgave yourself, I know. And I never forgave you either."

Cole pondered the notes given to him, especially the last one and its hidden message: I remained. *How can that be? They found partial skeletal remains. It just can't be.*

"Who are you?" Cole asked, though he already knew the answer.

From the shadow stepped a man in army green cargo pants, black boots and a black hoodie, and a black pistol of unknown type. The gun was extended and pointed at Cole's chest. In his other hand, a hand with only three fingers, he held a hunting knife with a jagged, eight-inch long blade.

Even with so many years gone by, Cole recognized the eyes and the face of Justin, filled with fury and revulsion.

"I can't believe you didn't figure it out sooner. You didn't actually think Lawrence would be able to do this. That bastard's long been dead, but I'm still around. Not without scars, of course." Justin revealed the underside of the hand holding the knife so Cole could clearly see the missing fingers.

"He did that to you? What a monster."

"Among other things. But a monster? Not sure about that. *You* ran away and left Kylie and me behind. And no one came to save us. So, who's the monster?" Justin's voice was growing more and more intense with each word, his anger bubbling.

Cole just shook his head, unable to defend his actions and still in shock that Justin was the man standing in front of him, a boy he thought had been dead for twenty years.

"So, what's the endgame here? You going to kill us all for a little revenge because of a bad decision I made when I was eleven years old?

You think that hasn't haunted me for this entire time?"

"Oh, I know what the years have done to you. I've watched you for a while now, sulking about, wasting your life. You got away, and yet you did nothing with it. That's almost a bigger slap in the face than leaving us behind.

"You see, Cole, I watched you at the cemetery for the past few years, and I actually admire your resolve to keep punishing yourself day after day, year after year. It truly is remarkable. But it's also a huge fuckin' waste of the memory of my sister. You saved your own life and gave up ours. And for what? For a slight, melancholy, worthless, loveless, pointless life. You might as well have died back then!"

"I know all this! You think I don't? I'm sick of this game. Just tell me how it ends and let's get it over with. I'm done."

"Okay. Let's do just that. Lawrence chose me and I'm glad he did, if for no other reason than to make you pay for your choices. That dirty, old bastard did awful, awful things to me, and to others, but I've done some pretty bad shit too, all because of you. So, here's what's gonna happen.

"First, I'm going to slide this knife over to you." Justin bent down, placed the knife on the floor, and kicked it over. "You're going to pick it up and use it to kill that little girl laying over there."

"There's no way I'm picking up that knife," Cole argued."

"Oh, I'm afraid you will. Because if you don't, I'm going to do very, very bad things to her before I slit both their throats, all right in front of you. Then I'll probably just torture you for a good, long while. How's that sound? At least this way, I'll let the boy live. You, on the other hand. Well, I haven't quite decided yet."

Cole shook his head and mouthed the word no. He quickly looked back to the kids who were still lying silent and still.

"You're going to know what it feels like to kill a sweet, little eight-year-old girl with a knife, just like he made me do," Justin's voice caught a slight quiver.

Not long after Cole escaped from the cabin -

After a short, unsuccessful chase of Cole, Lawrence arrived back at the cabin in a fit of rage. He aggressively pushed the already partially open door, shaking the entire place when it made contact with the wall behind it.

At the table, he leaned forward and planted both his hands down, breathing heavy and trying hard to calm down and think about his next move. He felt like he had the three children under control, but the simple mistake of leaving the key to the cabin on the table unattended would prove to unravel his whole life if he didn't react fast.

For months, he had worked to prepare a new location that would make his life easier, at least as far as travel time was concerned. Driving to and from the city twice a week to deal with his captives was taking its toll on him, and though he preferred not to move his operation under such duress, he knew the timetable had changed. Within a short time, Cole would find help, and eventually, he would lead the authorities back to the cabin.

Lucky for Lawrence, the property he had been using had no connection to him in any legal sense. The hunter's cabin was several miles off the beaten path and had long been abandoned by whomever owned it. He happened across it two years earlier while out hunting deer, and ever since then, he claimed it for his own, using it for sinister purposes.

The only thing missing was the front door, which he took care of by installing an old one from the warehouse owned by his family. He fell in love with the door upon seeing that green knob for the first time as a child, a time he wished he could forget, but the knob enchanted him nonetheless.

Within minutes, Lawrence made a decision about what to do with the cabin, but in the two-plus weeks since snatching Cole, Justin, and Kylie, he had made another decision as well. He would keep only one of them long term. With Cole's escape, there was one less option, although, within the first three days the children were there, he had already discovered his favorite, and it wasn't Cole.

In a scramble to make sure there was nothing on the property that could identify him, he cleared out any personal belongings, which wasn't much - some dishes, an old pair of boots, the gas-powered generator used to supply electricity to the cabin, a few tools, and most importantly to him, that strange metal and wood door with the emerald knob. He left the two, red gasoline-filled plastic containers just inside the door.

After the truck was fully loaded, he stepped over to the children and stood at the end of their mattresses, eyes locked on his choice. He released the cuff from Justin's wrist, placed an object into the boy's hand, then whispered instructions and a warning into his ear.

"I can't. She's my sister," Justin begged.

Lawrence cocked his arm and launched a powerful backhand into Justin's right cheek, knocking him to the ground.

"Don't argue with me boy! You know what

I'm capable of. Now get up and do it." He
grabbed the boy roughly by the arm and returned
him to his feet. "I'll be back in a second. Be quick
about it. We don't have much time."

Once satisfied Justin would do as instructed,
Lawrence picked up the first of the two
containers of gasoline and started to splash the
fluid around the edges of the room, leaving wet
splash marks on all the walls of the kitchen area,
the sink, the table and chairs, and the floor. He
tossed the empty container into the sink before
grabbing the second one.

Meanwhile, Justin looked at the blade, then
looked to his sister who had started to cry softly
when Lawrence struck her brother. She couldn't
bear to see him hurt anymore. Justin shook his
head.

"I can't," he whispered. "I can't." He thought
about plunging the blade into his own belly to
avoid killing his sister, but the idea of leaving her
behind with that devil sickened him, and it
wouldn't solve anything.

"Come here," Kylie whispered. She waved him
toward her and he complied. Even at her age,
Kylie had already figured out what the knife was
for. She could not foresee a happy ending for
herself but she held out hope for her big brother.

Justin stepped around to the left side of the
mattress and knelt down next to his sister,

holding the blade in front of his body and pointed right at her, the handle snug to his belly. He could not keep his hands steady.

As brave as ever, Kylie shifted her body to the edge of the bed and said, "It's okay, Justin. It's okay."

Justin vigorously shook his head.

"You have to. You have to or you'll never get free. Like Cole."

Justin knew she was right. If he was going to have any chance to live, he would have to do it. With the blade at the ready, his body refused to budge. He started to cry. Kylie cried with him.

She reached forward and put her arms at his elbows. "I love you, Justin. Tell mom and dad I love them too. And Fritzy. Give him a good petting for me," she said through heavy tears. "Now get away from him, anyway you can."

Without warning, she thrust her brother's arms toward her as hard as she could and simultaneously leaned forward, sending the blade into the right side of her abdomen, just below the ribcage. It slid down and lacerated her liver, among other things. She gasped. Her head fell to his shoulder.

Kylie spoke her finally words in his ear. "Run ... away. Like ... Cole." She faded into the sleep of angels, resting on the chest and shoulder of her big brother. She sacrificed herself so he may live, always courageous, brave until her last breath.

Justin balled. "No, Kylie! No!" He was in a state of shock at how fast it happened and in total disbelief. He let go of the blade and nudged her body away from his. She fell back and slumped sideways, bloodied and limp.

Lawrence peeked around the bamboo room divider to see if his chosen child had completed the chore. "Stand by this for a minute," he said as he pointed to the divider. "And stop crying or you'll get the same. And it won't be nearly so quick. I'll make sure you suffer. The pain will be ... unbearable."

Justin obeyed on both counts.

Lawrence repeated his splashing of gasoline across the walls and floors, the mattresses, and Kylie's body. He retrieved the knife, leaving behind the gas container to be burned with the rest. He smeared the blood from the blade onto the mattress.

The beast turned back to Justin. "We need them to think you both died here, so we're going to have to leave a little something behind ... from you. And it's gonna hurt like hell."

Justin had no idea what that meant.

"Come here," Lawrence demanded.

Justin did as he was told. Lawrence grabbed the two smallest fingers on Justin's right hand, and with the knife, severed them from his hand like a man with experience doing it. The vicious butchering was over in five seconds. Justin only screamed after, the event too quick for him to even react. His face went white, sweat pouring from everywhere. Blood splattered and dripped on the floor at their feet.

Lawrence had made a makeshift torch out of the speared squirrel carcass, wrapping the top in an old t-shirt and dousing it in gasoline. He sheathed the knife, picking up the torch and a lighter from the table. With a flick of the lighter, he ignited the torch and walked back to Justin.

"Give me your hand," Lawrence commanded. "You don't want to bleed to death."

Justin robotically put his bloody and damaged hand forward. Lawrence grabbed the boy's wrist and held it tight as he cauterized the wound with the fire of the torch.

Justin whelped and almost passed out from the pain, but somehow did not, managing to stay on his feet.

"You did good boy. Now let's get out of here before the police show up." Lawrence ushered Justin out the door, who was grasping the side of his injured hand. He kept the boy in view at all times.

Just as Lawrence was about to toss the torch back through the open doorway, he remembered he had a spare key to the door he had already removed, hidden under a rock a few feet from where they stood. He kicked the rock over and picked up the key, placing it in one of his back pockets.

With nothing else left to do, he launched the torch inside.

In just under an hour since Cole ran away, Lawrence had cleared out the cabin and was sitting in his truck alongside Justin, watching the blaze send smoke and flame into the air, charred wood crumbling and flesh burning.

Justin sat mostly silent, tears streaming from both eyes behind a mix of muffled sobbing and whimpering. Adrenaline was taking care of his pain, for the moment, and with no desire to engage the wrath of his tormentor, he did the best job imaginable at keeping quiet, the trauma of the past ten minutes burning deep into his soul.

Once satisfied the fire would do its job, Lawrence drove away from the property for the last time. The trampled path of two grooves snaked its way through the mass of trees surrounding the property, eventually leading to a remote country road. Their destination - a location specifically chosen for his games of torture and dominance. It would become the home for the wretched child sitting next to him, a child reborn into death and blood.

That kind of rebirth, however, had already taken place before, altogether the same, yet altogether different. Lawrence Kranski, the kidnapper, the master, the devil, was a child of similar creation - from pain and suffering and hate. Another link in the chain of abuse had been added, another cycle of violence had only just begun.

***

Cole stood shocked and dismayed by the truth of that day so long ago. The details leading up to the fire were known only to Justin and Lawrence.

"But you didn't know any of that, did you? How could you? No one knew."

Cole remained still, dumbfounded.

"He came back and decided he was going to burn it all down, but he could only keep one of us." Justin raised his right index finger. "Just one. His favorite.

"He made me ... cut her," the words squeaked out. "Kylie, my little sister, was brave. Braver than me. Braver than you. She said it would be okay. She said I could get out. Like Cole. Like you!" The anger churned. "Yeah, right," he said through gritted teeth. "Like Cole. A big, chickenshit coward who saved his own ass, AND LEFT US BEHIND!" He took two deep breaths. "You left us for that fucking bastard to rape and torture! YOU DID THIS! YOU, COLE! YOU!"

"I'm sorry!" Cole shouted. "I didn't know any of that. I was scared. I was a fuckin' kid! And you're right, I was a coward. I only thought of myself and I've lived every day for the last twenty years with that on my back. I would trade my life for Kylie's ... or for yours."

"But you can't!" Justin interrupted.

"No, no I can't, but I would do it in a second if I could. I can't make a different choice and rewrite history. And I deserve your wrath and Kylie deserves vengeance. What more can I do?"

"You can kill that girl and know what it's like to be me, just for one minute. Then you'll know real pain."

"No, Justin! I'll do one better, because making me into you is not going to bring her back, and it won't change what you've become. I'm going to make a better choice this time and end the cycle with you, Justin."

"You will do it! You stick that fucking knife in her belly or you're all going to die, slow and painful!"

"No! It ends ... here!" Cole pointed firmly to the ground with fire in his eyes. He summoned a courage he believed did not exist, a power he thought had been taken from him as a boy. *No more*, he thought. *No more, no more, no more. Even if*

I die trying, I came into this room to save those kids, and goddamn it, that is exactly what I intend to do.

"Time's up. Do it now or I shoot you in the kneecap and I'll start with her." Justin had turned into a man of rage and revenge. He wanted Cole to experience something similar to what he had twenty years before, and he refused to give up on the idea.

"I don't think you're going to shoot me at all. That would mess up your plan, and you don't want that."

"Don't tell me what I will or will not do. You don't have the first clue what I want or what I'm capable of. Don't test me! Pick up the knife and do as you're told." His words seethed with hate.

Cole made up his mind. He only hoped he understood Justin more than Justin understood himself. Cole reached down, slow, and picked up the knife, a frightening looking blade that reminded him of a crocodile's bottom jaw.

In order for Justin to accomplish what he set out to do, which was to make Cole feel the same way he did, he couldn't very well shoot Cole. That would mess up the whole plan, and Cole was counting on that fact. His life depended on it.

"Okay, Justin. Let's just get this over with." Cole turned his back to Justin and stepped over to the end of the bed nearest the girl. "Get over here. I'm only going to do this once, then you'll let the boy go and this will all be over."

Justin inched closer, gun at the ready and pointed right at Cole's lower back, the muzzle within two feet of him.

Suddenly, Cole swung his left arm around, slamming the large blade into the side of the gun, dislodging it from Justin's hand and sending it across the room. Justin didn't see it coming and wasn't quite sure how to react.

At first, they both just stood there, looking into each other's eyes for clues. Cole held the knife in front of him and witnessed a look in Justin's eyes that he could not entirely quantify, yet somehow, he fully understood what it meant. Cole shook his head to dissuade him but it was too late.

Justin charged Cole, who did nothing but stand firm, allowing the blade of the knife to tear open Justin's abdomen, thrashing the skin and his entrails as he twisted in agony. The blood coated Cole's hand and the bottom of his shirt before he let loose the handle.

Justin grabbed the handle of the knife with both hands and looked Cole dead in the eyes.

"We're the same ... now." Justin choked on the blood rising from his stomach. "You and me, we're the..." Justin fell hard to his knees, the crack of bone on concrete unnerving Cole and causing a shiver.

Cole closed his eyes and started to cry with sadness and relief. Justin was dead, and he and the kids were alive. That was more than he expected.

He knelt down to the body and closed Justin's eyelids. "I'm sorry it had to end this way. Be at peace. Be with Kylie."

Cole searched the pockets of Justin and found a cell phone. He turned in the direction of the children.

"If you can hear me, wait here. I'm going to go figure out where we are and call the police. I'll be right back."

He rushed out of the room, down the hall, and out of the exit door. His chest heaved from the exertion. He inhaled short, hurried breaths trying to get enough air.

The afternoon light blinded him for a few seconds, but once his vision fully returned, he dialed 9-1-1 and began trying to figure out where they were located. He hoped the GPS of the phone could be used by the police. After looking around, he didn't recognize the area.

While the phone rang, he looked over the railing of the balcony he came out on, noting he was on the second floor of a two-story building. The exterior was faded red brick. Down near the corner of the building and bolted to the brick just to Cole's right was a large gold-plated and chipped number 9. He thought about what kind of building would have a giant number like that. A firehouse?

"This is Lauren with Lansing 9-1-1. What's your emergency?"

"My name ... is Cole Redman. I just killed ... a guy ... who was holding ... some kids captive." He paused to catch his breath.

"Sir, did you say you just killed a guy?"

"Yes."

"And he was holding some kids captive? How many?"

"Yes. Two. A boy and a girl, maybe ... eight and ten years old. They were in the newspaper."

"Are you or the children injured?"

"I'm not. They look okay. I think they were drugged. I don't know where we are. I think it might be an old firehouse. There's a large, gold number nine on the side of the building, but I don't recognize the neighborhood."

"I have your location from the phone you're using. I'm sending the police and an ambulance to your location. Are you in the building or outside?"

"I'm out on a balcony on the second floor."

"Good. Stay there and signal the authorities when they arrive."

"Okay. Thank you."

"You're welcome. Just stay on the line until help gets there. Everything is going to be fine."

"Thank you."

The first officer arrived in less than two minutes, the paramedics and more police cruisers arrived another two minutes after that. Cole waved them in from the balcony. They broke the front door down to gain entry.

Cole returned to be with the children while waiting for the authorities to find them on the second floor. When they did, Cole was asked to stand aside while the paramedics dealt with the children. Even though he was covered in blood, he had informed the paramedics he was not injured. Cole waited by the door, as far away from Justin as he could be and still be in the room.

The usual procedures took place. The children were put on gurneys and taken to the hospital, crime scene investigators began examining the scene, and Cole was taken downstairs by a uniformed officer to be questioned by a detective that was in route to the scene.

15

Saturday, November 10th, 2012 – 7:57 p.m.
Lansing, Michigan

After spending four hours at the police station answering questions and telling the entire story of how he came to be at the old firehouse and his relationship to Justin, Cole was allowed to go home.

For the first time ever, Cole spilled the beans of his experience, starting with the truth about his behavior during Detective Jebsen's questioning twenty years earlier, the deceit he authored, and how it affected his life. The reaction from the detectives was of astonishment and disbelief, not because of what Cole did but at how it still affected him. It was made clear to Cole, that no matter what he had told the police as an eleven-year-old boy, he could not have saved Kylie, or Justin for that matter. The timing was off. Even as Cole was being questioned from his hospital bed the first time by Jeb, the cabin had already been burned and no one even reported the large smoke stack for hours afterward. By the time he was discovered on the side of the road, it was too late. Kylie was dead and Justin may as well have been.

Cole's guilt did not immediately subside, even facing those facts. Too many years and too many memories were in place to dismiss so easily. Only time and a gradual remaking of his memories would revise the history. He held out hope that with an ever-loosening grip of his own vision of the past, and with enough retellings of the story, the truth would settle in.

Cole exited the backseat of the squad car belonging to Officer Brett Langley, who was kind enough to give him a ride home. Brett rolled down the passenger window and called to Cole.

"You're going to be okay, Cole," the officer said.

Cole stopped, turned, and crouched down to see the officer. "I know."

"Give somebody you know a call, be around

people as much as you can. It'll make you feel better. Trust me."

"Thanks, Officer. I'll do that. 'preciate the ride home," Cole finished with a wave. He turned back to the house.

Officer Langley put the window back up and drove away.

Cole dug into his pocket and pulled out his keys, luckily found at the scene. He located the one for the front door, even in the dark, as it was the only one with a square head. He inserted the key in the lock and turned it, but for reasons unknown to him, he couldn't immediately push the door open. He never thought he would see his house again. Being back there was a little surreal at first. The biggest sense of relief he had ever felt washed over him.

He knew a shower and the softness of his own bed were waiting inside, so he mustered the strength to go in. In the dark, he walked straight through to the kitchen. He flicked the light switch to his right, and the cool, white glow of the recessed lights in the ceiling brought the room to life.

Sheer terror held his legs still, his hands trembling at the sight of a six by nine-inch manila envelope sitting on the edge of his kitchen table. The words in red ink left no doubt as to the person responsible.

Through quivering lips, Cole said, "He's dead. I killed him myself not six hours ago. How could this be here?" The emotional side of his brain almost sent him running away, but suddenly, the logical side took over. "Oh, duh. He must have left this sometime between when he kidnapped me and when I escaped the room. That's the only explanation. Calm down, Cole. I guess even *he* thought I would make it out alive." Cole's body and mind relaxed. He was still curious what the envelope held. After all, it would be the last words of Justin.

Cole stepped to the table and picked up envelope number five. It had the usual stuff written on the front in red marker: Every assist comes with a price. This one costs you: (HEAT, FOOD, WATER, LIFE) 1 ...

The words heat, food, and water each had the red X over them. The word life was circled multiple times.

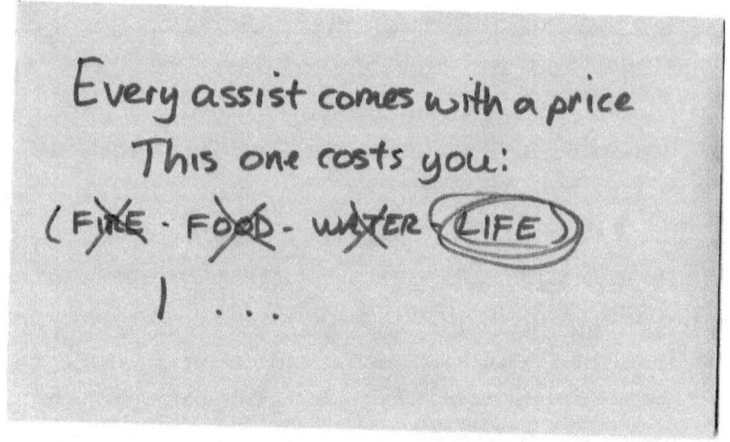

One thing that stood out about the final envelope was the contents. It was puffed up instead of being flat like the others. Clearly, it contained something more than just a piece of paper and it crunched when he squeezed it. He carefully opened the clasp and dumped the contents onto the table. Out fell the remnants of twenty red trillium leaves collected by Justin from his own grave marker each year after Cole left the cemetery, along with the usual single piece of bi-folded copy paper.

Lawrence, though twisted by his horrible life experiences, was not entirely without empathy. Once he heard about the funeral for Kylie and Justin, he took Justin there each year on the date of the original burial, several days after Cole's visit each year, which happened to be on the anniversary of his own escape rather than the funeral itself.

Justin noticed the odd petals present near the bottom of the grave markers the first time he visited and knew they were out of place, like someone had put them there. Knowing his own grave marker to be false, he took the one from his own stone and kept it in a plastic baggie, and did that for twenty straight years. When he later found out it was Cole who was leaving the petals, he could barely believe the connection.

With the shake in his hands back, Cole picked up the letter and read it aloud, "coWard. you once again made a cHoice tO save yourself. I Sure hopE you can liVe wIth that. Liar." There were three question marks below the message.

"Who is evil?" Cole whispered the words imbedded in the message.

coWard. you once again made a cHoice tO save

yourself. I Sure hopE you can liVe wIth that. Liar.

???

Cole closed his eyes and remembered the final moments of Justin's life. A single tear fell down the left side of his cheek and onto his jacket. He rubbed his jaw line using the thumb and index finger of his free hand, and reopened his eyes, fixing his gaze at the words on the page. He shook his head in defiance of the underlying message.

"No. I'm not evil."

Cole stuffed the piece of paper back in the envelope, scraped the petals back in too, pulled a book of matches from one of his kitchen drawers, struck a match, and set the envelope on fire, placing it in the sink to watch it burn.

"And neither were you."

ABOUT THE AUTHOR

Richard is the author of *Kill Academy* (2017), the exciting new action/suspense/thriller and the first book in a planned trilogy. His previous works include *RejectGuy99* (2015), *A Room Full of Keys* (2013), and *Neither Snow, Nor Rain, Nor Zombie Infection* (2012).

He currently lives in Central Illinois with his wife Amy and Cavachon Padraig. When he's not reading and writing, he spends his time playing disc golf and pickleball, doing DIY projects, playing videogames, watching movies, and hosting amazing cookouts and parties.

www.richardapowellii.com

A Room Full Of Keys